IVORY BLOOD

HENRY PUMPKINCLAW

TABLE OF CONTENTS

PROLOGUE

The hunter steadied his gun, boots sinking deeper into the muddy ground with wet grime climbing up to their laces. Normally the forest would be teaming with loud calls and the chatter of local wild life but, instead, it was filled with dreadful silence. He felt the odd atmosphere and understood not a predator alive could provoke the intense stillness around him, at least not one that he ever saw.

Heal to toe he stepped carefully through the rain forest with his raised elephant gun in hand, pushing aside branches and giant leaves with soft ease and ghost like movements.

Water dripped onto his leather jacket and hat from the dense forest canopy, the dark concealing the sun's rays as precious light filtered through broken fragments from above, forcing him to wait patiently after each step-in order to allow his sight to readjust.

The curious silence preoccupied his thoughts distracting his attention from the task at hand. He had to remind himself repeatedly to hush his wandering mind and to concentrate on tracking the target he had engaged.

Earlier, when the sun was somewhere else in the sky, the hunter observed an adolescent elephant just a few meters away from the position he currently held. Something startled the youngling who sought safety further into the protection of the forest escaping from the man's view. Following its path by tracks and broken leaves the hunter was able to pinpoint the area where he predicted his prey began to lose energy and seek rest.

The smell of blood entered his nostrils, he was all too familiar with its coppery scent. Cautious and guarded he moved on, sensing the stench of death mixed with fresh blood. The odor, increasing and inescapable, the shifting wind, carried the scent directing the hunter.

Adjusting his speed to quiet any excessive noise from his movement, the remaining light almost immediately disappeared forcing him to pause in order to gain his bearings. A small fragmented beam of sun returned through an exposed opening from the canopy revealing a stain at the end of his rifle.

The red smear ran the entire length of his gun to where his hand rested, fresh blood dripped from his sleeve onto his muddy boot. With his eyes attuned to the change of light he saw that the brush he was passing through was covered with large patches of a crimson sheen.

After what felt like an eternity in eerie silence, the hush was broken by a frightening sound; it was unmistakably something chewing on bone and flesh.

His head cried for his feet to step backward and retreat, but, despite his pleading intuition, curiosity pushed him forward into a clearing where he saw the most awful thing he could ever have imagined.

At first it didn't make any sense, but when the confusion lifted, the hunter began to process and conceptualize what was laid before him: massacred carcasses of what appeared to be hundreds of dead elephants sprawled everywhere around the clearing; the blood in the air combined with the stench of decay watering his eyes while he tried to distinguish the variation from freshly killed to half rotten corpses; and scattered among the hulking remains, endless bone fragments and pieces of fleshy appendages making it impossible to tell exactly how many there were.

Small amounts of light from behind him allowed his eyes to gain fragile sight in the utter blackness. Stepping further into the clearing he could feel brittle bones crunching under his heavy weight, soft flesh giving way to the pressure of his boot that sent a surge of disgust through his body, beginning at his feet seconds before residual fear kicked in.

Looking around he saw movement on the other side of the clearing, close to the forest edge. A massive creature was leaning forward with its front legs bent engorging on the soft tissue of what appeared to be the remains of a juvenile elephant.

Though the hunter's mind instantly cried that it was impossible, he knew what it was. The immense trunk protruding from its face, the huge bone tusks on the side of its bloody gaping maw…. it was unquestionable.

As he stood in a frozen state of shock, he saw it lift a large tusk and crashed it down on the lifeless head of the adolescent, emitting the most horrible sound, echoing through the clearing. The tusk raised dripping with clumps of blood and brain matter stuck to the ivory, then the monster used its trunk to pick up the shattered pieces feeding with a ravenous hunger.

The hunter proclaimed, horrified, "Grootslang."

The horror instantly stopped, lifting its head looking directly at the man, the hunter could almost make out a pinpoint spot of red in the center of its deep black eyes.

Stories from shaman are shared in various villages across the continent. They tell of primordial demons as old as the world itself, too powerful even for the gods so they were banished into a bottomless pit. Here he was, in the behemoth's liar staring at a creature even the gods feared.

The moment of recognition was over. Once he locked into those heinous and incessant eyes the remnant of his sanity was drained. The scream he emitted was unanswered by the jungle, for that piece of the forest stood utterly still in fear as another victim was claimed by one of its awful secrets.

1

London 1890

In the office of The Daily Guardian John Alpert hunched over his desk piecing together the scraps of telegraphs he had collected from the home office over the past week. The information was displayed in front of him like a disorganized puzzle. Each section held a few sentences he was attempting to connect into a larger story that he could present to his editor before his deadline.

The office was covered in blackness except for the globe of light emitted by his personal oil lamp; he felt the cold solitude surrounding his coworker's shadowed desks.

The only sound in the room was that of distant thunder accompanied by the rain tapping against the glass of the street-facing windows.

"Famed Explorer Missing in Free State of Congo" read the bold print, the smaller text bellow described in further detail the missing person's exploits and last known whereabouts, before being reported lost by the contracted company that sent him into that region.

John assumed the company, in all likelihood was not concerned with the man's wellbeing but was just following protocol, to file an insurance claim against the money they had lost on the contract's deposit.

John Alpert was currently tasked, by his superiors, to follow up with the ongoing European turmoil of the West African Colonies. The previous year he had won commendation and notoriety for writing a significant piece on the impact of the West African Conference, specifically on the trade agreements precedingly arranged. Recent developments exposed a forthcoming feud between France and Her Majesty's England regarding expansion into undeclared regions of the dark continent, and though his fellow journalists said there was nothing to report he trusted his own instincts.

A gloved hand grasped his shoulder and John quickly turned to find his sister's husband Michael Allen standing behind him with a cheerful grin. His hat and coat were drenched from being outside in the rain, pools of water forming on the wooden floor boards at his feet.

"What news heralds form the Guardian at this hour John?"

Michael removed his wet hat and took off his gloves placing both on the desk opposite from John's. He pulled out the chair belonging to the same desk that accompanied it and sat across from his old friend.

Michael and John had known each other from childhood, both had graduated from Cambridge. John studied writing and journalism, while Michael concentrated on business. Though their subjects were distinct both men stayed in constant contact throughout their years at University.

After Cambridge, Michael and John returned to the outskirts of London where Michael was hired as the manager of a telegraph station which happened to be in the same location where John's sister Margaret, was working. After a brief courtship Michael and Margaret were married, making Michael more than a close friend, he became family. Michael would leave the telegraph business and, through connections he had made, began work in futures trading and commodities, specifically oils.

"Nothing of interest, just piecing together a follow up from a previous article I had written," replied John who turned away from his friend organizing the disheveled papers preparing to leave for the night.

Michael stood up and looked over John's shoulder at the scraps of telegraphs, he leaned in and picked up the last one his friend was just holding looking it over. John turned his head and watched Michael's eyes dart left to right as he absorbed the information on the telegraph.

"This fellow is missing in the Congo Free State?" asked Michael holding out the telegraph for John to take.

"It is believed so. The communique was sent out by the insurer of the company in which he was employed. I assume they want to avoid any financial responsibility," replied John occupied with his current task.

"Do you think some savage man eater or beast was at hand?" further inquired Michael.

"I doubt it. The most logical explanation is, that he was wounded by a native army or warring faction. Or, he could have fallen, suffered from a horrid infection, and he is decomposing in some dark corner of Africa."

"Morbid John," Michael said with a disgusted grimace.

"Well, Africa is full of the macabre and bleak," John said looking up at Michael from his chair.

"And that is exactly why I stay in England, where the only cheerless quality one needs to worry about is terrible tea," Michael replied with a slight titter.

"There is so much unknown about the region, much we need to understand," John said waving his hands over his desk acknowledging all the papers before him.

Michael removed a folded paper from the inside of his coat pocket and held it out to John who at first stared at it in puzzlement before taking it in his hands and carefully opening it.

"What is this?" John inquired with confusion.

"The Colonial office in Westminster has requested a meeting with you and me. It does not say much but, coincidentally, it explains that your political knowledge of the colonies and my experience in trade is needed," said Michael.

"Is the letter is addressed to both of us?" asked John further perplexed.

"That is correct old friend. I am sure if you bothered to go home instead of spending all of your time here you would find one waiting for you," Michael jabbed.

"When do they expect our presence?" John asked glancing over the letter

"Three days from today. If you would like, you could stay in the guest room and we could leave together by train," Michael replied.

"You already agreed on my behalf?" asked John flatly.

"I am sorry old boy but I do not imagine this is an optional meeting and Her Majesty's Government does not wait for inquiry," argued Michael.

"No, I cannot imagine on both terms," John said now carefully reading over the paper.

They sat in silence, Michael patiently standing by as John read the letter over a few more times, futilely attempting to reveal some secret meaning as to what this could possibly pertain to.

Michael impatiently stood up, picked his hat and gloves off the desk then pushed the chair back to its original spot.

"Come along now. Margaret expects your company tonight and we both know she is even more unforgiving than the government," said Michael.

John stood up from his desk and walked over to the hanger on the wall removing his own coat and hat. While putting them on he waited by his desk until his friend opened the office door allowing in light, from gas fixtures in the hall, extinguishing his own desk lamp.

- - - -

They took a horse drawn carriage meant for two across town to the area of London where Michael and Margaret lived. The Allen's could afford to reside in the upper middle-class area in a terraced regency style house. Built with brick, their home was two stories with a windowed attic under a slanted slate roof that during the summer revealed a beautiful garden.

By the time their carriage approached the house the rain slowed to a steady drizzle. As the men entered the warm home, they could hear Margaret calling for their servant Nancy to help them remove their coats and make sure the "boys" (as she referred to them) did not get the floor too wet.

Nancy was a middle-aged woman, employed by John's sister and brother-in-law for the past five years. She had her own accommodations located in the rear right corner of the house. Nancy came over to the two men with confidence yet held a steady reserved approach, acknowledging silently her respected employer.

She helped remove Michael's coat and then he passed to her his hat and gloves. John took off his outer garments and handed them to Nancy who held the apparel steadily with both arms.

"Nancy, will you start a fire for John and I in the study?" asked Michael.

"It is already set for you sir at the request of Mrs. Allen," answered Nancy.

"That is splendid, and where is Mrs. Allen?" Michael asked with a continuously pleasant tone.

"Upstairs getting ready for dinner Mr. Allen."

"Wonderful," said Michael "Come along John, let us have a drink before the feast. Nancy please inform us when dinner is ready."

"Of course, sir," Nancy replied with slight bend of her knee, before heading down the hall to hang up the damp coats in the closet.

Michael and John were about to set off into the study to warm themselves in front of the fire before Margaret presented herself at the top of the stairs.

"My boys will not be going anywhere without saying hello to their lady first," she called down to them.

Margaret stood at the top of the carpeted steps, a woman in her early 30's with auburn hair curled down lightly over her shoulders wearing a radiant teal dress.

She made her way down, elegantly to the entrance floor and smiled at both of them hugging each as well as giving them a kiss on the cheek.

"John I am so glad you agreed to dinner," she said embracing her brother.

"I was told it was a requirement," John answered teasing his sister on her predictable nature.

John was two years Margaret's senior, as children they were not inseparable but it was not uncommon to see John partaking in Margaret's games or John permitting her to tag along in his boyish adventures. When Michael approached John on the subject of seeing his sister on a romantic level, it gladdened his heart that Margaret found such an honorable man to care for her, not that Margaret needed a man.

She was much like their mother, independent in style and class; quick to brush off the social standards of an obedient and submissive women.

When Margaret finished with primary school, she was eager to enter the work force. With more and more openings in telegraphic work there were opportunities for young women to fill the need. Margaret jumped on the opportunity.

John always felt her ambitious character was what attracted Michael to Margaret in the first place, her drive to be self-sufficient, her total rejection of being perceived as weak and helpless.

After John and Michael sat for a time in front of the fire enjoying a pre-dinner cognac, Nancy came to the study to announce that the first course was about to be served. The men entered the Dining room where a table that could comfortably seat eight, was set for three. An unused candelabra was placed in the center of the table.

It was common in many houses of the Allens' stature to have electric lamps throughout. Since they could be finicky, many households kept multiple candelabras in case of an outage. The Allens' luckily never experienced such disruptions.

Michael, Margaret and John had a glass of wine with the first course of sweat breads and peas. After Nancy cleared the plates, she brought out the main course of Veal Cutlets, stuffed tomatoes and a dish of fried artichokes which John couldn't help but consume in an unconventional ferocious manner.

"This is fantastic! What is this dish called?" asked John in between helpings.

"It is called Gouffe. A creation by the brother of Queen Victoria's head pastry chef Alphonse," Margaret said smiling with a bit of gloat at her brother's enjoyment.

"How did you come about this recipe?" inquired John eagerly.

"The credit must be given to Nancy. She brought to my attention a recent French cook book translated into English. This dish is fancied by the Lords and Ladies of the Upper class," Margaret replied attempting to control the level of boasting in her voice.

"The French! Their continuous naked expansion and aggression into Her Majesty' colonial regions should be met with a swift hand," scoffed Michael before taking a sip of his wine.

"You sound like one of my editors," John replied looking towards Michael.

"Their blatant attempts at linking the Nile and Niger interlope on our trade routes and completely go against the principles agreed upon in the West African Conference," retorted Michael.

"Michael, I am astonished at your recounting of the rhetorical jargon being used by Parliament," said John with a swift counter.

"Rhetorical Jargon? Please elaborate on how the validity of their behavior is rhetorical jargon?" Michael asked holding his glass of wine.

"The reports from military officials in the area say nothing of aggressive action on part of the French army. Actually, they are contrary to that, and state the contact between the two armies is most civil," John replied unflinchingly.

"Then why are the papers-such as your very own Guardian I may add- displaying a picture of oncoming dissension in East Africa?" pushed back Michael.

John stared at his friend unblinking "Perhaps our own expansive agenda to connect southern colonies to eastern colonies."

Michael replied with a smirk of enjoyment. "You should be careful with that sort of talk John, especially outside of this house. One could accuse you of blasphemy against The Crown."

"All I am insinuating my old friend is that everyone has a motive when it comes to political strife. Maybe your very own trade concerns have more to do with your investment in Palm oils and free trade routes than nationalistic ideals of France against England," John continued.

"You once again display my hypocrisy for all to see. Well done old boy," Michael said lightly slamming his hand down on the table.

"Well I have had enough of watching you both displaying your manhood from across the table. John will you be staying the night?" interrupted Margaret.

"I am sorry dear sister but I am unable to," John said looking in Margaret's direction.

"However, he will be staying with us Thursday evening. We must attend an important meeting in Westminster. John agreed to have dinner with us the night before and play games," Michael said looking to John for agreement.

"Fantastic news. You will not be leaving tonight before desert, will you? Nancy has prepared a berry toast that compliments the wine," Insisted Margaret.

"Sounds wonderful," said John smiling at his sister.

"And I have a cigar that compliments it all, along with more prodding on your favoritism of French politics," teased Michael.

"That sounds dreadful Michael, but as a dutiful guest I will oblige," John joked.

All three picked up their glasses in a silent toast and took a sip of the wine. Outside the rain picked up again and a continuous clap of thunder filled the silence while they waited for Nancy to serve desert.

- - - -

The Office of Colonial Development was in the building for Foreign and Provincial Affairs located in Westminster. It was a large gray stone structure taking up most of the block between Horse Guards Road and Chambers Street. John and Michael arrived a half hour early and were directed into a large conference room with a table that could comfortably seat nine people. After waiting until quarter past the hour, three men walked into the room and sat on the opposite side of the table from John and Michael.

All sported either black or grey blazers, vests and neck ties, giving off the air of obvious government officials, resonating a sense of respectability. Michael fancied himself as a man who knew how to dress appropriately but could not help but admire their suits. The man in the middle had a full black beard while the other two had mustaches and side burns.

"Good day gentleman, I am William Robert, Under Secretary of State. Let me introduce you to Herman Rogers and Fredric Meade. They are resident members on the Board of Trade and Plantation," the man in the middle said with a strong sense of self confidence.

"My name is Michael Allen and this is my long-time compatriot and brother-in-law John Alpert," Michael responded standing up shaking each man's hand. John repeated the appropriate gesture followed by a silent head nod.

"Gentleman, we have asked you here today on the chance that you could assist us with an increasingly difficult international situation," said Mr. Roberts.

"What situation might that be?" asked John coolly.

"For one, Mr. Alpert, we are well versed on your coverage of the Berlin Conference. Your articles have caught the attention of many in Parliament. Your in-depth understanding of current events in colonial African are most impressive," said Mr. Roberts.

"We are also aware of Mr. Allen's application for permits to import rubber productions from South America," asked Mr. Meade.

John was caught off guard, he assumed they were here for nothing more than a discussion of his contacts in the field. Now, he was worried that his longtime friend had entangled him in a political deal that could somehow land them both in legal peril.

"Are we under inquiry? I have broken no laws pertaining to my current permit request. That being said, John has no previous knowledge or financial connection to said ventures," Michael responded in a slightly defensive tone.

"You are under no inquiry, Mr. Allen, I can assure you of that," Mr. Roberts insisted.

"Mr. Alpert, are you familiar with the articles established six years ago in Berlin?" asked Mr. Rogers.

"I have some knowledge of the details outlined in the accords," answered John now a little more relaxed.

"Then you are aware of the consensus to abolish the slave trade, along with forced labor, in the African colonial region?" continued Mr. Rogers.

"It was a vote in Berlin, based upon European public sentiment, to discontinue persecution of natives in the colonies," replied John.

"That is correct. There is however, one nation that is of a concern. It is believed King Leopold of Belgium still utilizes forced labor and practices mass executions in the Congo Free State, which is in direct violation of the agreed upon pact," elaborated Rogers.

"He originally agreed to end all further slavery in the region and to cooperate in ending Arabic slave trading. However, Leopold pushed taxation on exports in defiance of the agreement," Mr. Roberts interjected.

"Has this not been brought to the attention of other nations at the conference?" asked John.

"Our growing tensions with France put us in the unfortunate political position of having to avoid any further disputes. We fear there will be pushback by the French on the grounds of raising false accusations," said Mr. Meade.

"The Belgian government will defend its Crown and without solid evidence we are unable to raise an objection to the illicit tariffs," Mr. Rogers said with a solemn tone.

"So, you need substantial evidence before you can raise an international outcry. I assume that is where our involvement comes into play," said Michael leaning back in his chair.

"Our proposition is to contract with both of you as operatives. We need you to go in under the guise of sovereign executives from a mock South American rubber company seeking to expand operations," replied Mr. Roberts.

"We believe an individual of interest is one Max Gaston Gerlache."

He reached to the floor between himself and Mr. Meade, picking up a rectangular briefcase. Opening the case William Roberts took out a stack of folders, placing them on the desk.

He then opened the top folder taking out a sheet of paper and passed it to Michael and John. It was a profile, with a small black and white picture loosely fastened at the top left corner of Max Gerlache.

"He is an untitled Belgian noble and has been reported by sources to be a key figure propped up in the Congo Basin by King Leopold himself," continued Roberts.

The picture was grainy and judging by it alone you would not assume the man was highborn. He sported a thick black mustache which curled up in pointy ends to his cheeks. His hair, visible under a safari styled hat appeared white. His cloths were appropriate for African temperatures: a thin white shirt, grey colored vest and black pants.

"Gerlache owns multiple rubber plantations. Also he has deep connections in the ivory trade. Our real area of interest is his association with the International African Association and his close ties to a Captain Leon Roger of the Force Publique," said Mr. Roberts.

"Pardon me, but you did say Force Publique?" John asked placing the paper on the table and giving the men across from him a hard look.

Michael turned his head to face John, waiting for him to shed some light on the information that everyone at the table held except him.

"What is the Force Publique?" Michael asked, first looking at John then directing his eyes to the others.

"Officially, a private army. Their oppressive techniques in the region are infamous. Reports by foreign missionaries of rape and physical abuse are renowned along with other acts I dare not mention," John replied with a hushed tone.

Mr. Roberts turned a page in the folder revealing another profile with a picture attached to the corner. It was without question, Captain Leon Roger, sporting a white military suit, without accommodations, and a white brimmed hat with a gold emblem in the center. The most notable feature of Captain Roger's clean-shaven face was the deep anger in his eyes. It was clear even by this coarse image, that the man held a lot of hate. The moment John saw the photograph, he knew he never to cross paths with the individual in it.

"The Force Publique was originally created to enforce rubber quotas. Even though reports of their heinous actions are notorious, the Belgium government denies all of it. King Leopold maintains that the Force Publique is the primary tool used for eradication of the slave trade, contrary to reputation," Mr. Roberts elaborated "we believe that Captain Roger has parted with the Force Publique and is now providing his private services to Gerlache."

"Let us be very clear then. Our purpose is to engage Max Gerlache under the facade of South American rubber barons. Then we are to obtain proof of illicit operations by Gerlache and this Captain Roger?" Michael asked without blinking.

"That is correct, Mr. Allen. We will provide the finances necessary to make the trip there as well as your return journey home. Accounts will be set in an Amazonian bank account under the name Peruvian National Company for fiscal cover to support your story for verification," said Mr. Mead.

"You will be allotted a third of the agreed upon consignment deposited in your accounts here in England prior to departure. The balance will be dispensed upon your return on the condition that you provide us with the proof we require," Mr. Roberts continued.

"What standard of confirmation is required?" John asked with a suspicious look.

"Photographs would be the most valuable. Though we understand they would also be the most difficult to obtain. Also a deposition from any individual willing to return with you in exchange for asylum, preferably with close ties to Gerlache or Leopold. You would need to acquire the assistance of that individual while minimizing the risk of revealing your true nature. In addition your detailed accounts, accompanied by journal notes, would be of value," replied Mr. Rogers.

"May ask why both of us were chosen?" pressed John.

"Your eye for detail, Mr. Alpert. Also, the fact that both of you are admired but not connected with any government office. A stipulation with the agreement is you may be called upon to testify before an international committee on behalf of Parliament," said Mr. Roberts.

"Mr. Allen's knowledge of rubber production and import trade are essential to creating a believable front," spoke Mr. Meade.

"May we discuss this in private gentleman?" asked John with a quiet sense of doubt.

"Please by all means, we will step outside," said Rogers.

The three men stood up from their chairs, nodded their heads to John and Michael and exited the double wooden doors behind them. They left their folders behind leaving John to look through the profiles. He attempted to read Gerlache's profile but was continuously drawn back to the picture of Captain Roger. The thought of going undercover under a false identity was exciting, to say to say the least, but the notion of confronting this man was enough to cool his rising energy and ice any desire for adventure.

Michael spoke first, "I know that look John."

"We are venturing into the unknown, Michael. The stories I have heard, what if our cover is blown, they will kill us for sure?" John said pleadingly.

"No reward is without necessary risk," said Michael.

"That being said, we have much to lose. What do you think Margaret would say?" asked John.

"I am not one to assume what Margaret would say. Your sister is unpredictable, but, if she were in our shoes, I would like to think she would accept."

John turned to look at his friend, the gleam in Michael's eyes was that of a young man seeking adventure. If only he knew the darker truths that John understood. But John did not want to be the one to extinguish the promise of this task.

"If I were to go in this alone my refusal would be guaranteed," John stated.

They locked eyes and the agreement was unanimous. Michael stood from his chair and walked up to the double doors opening them up revealing the three men huddled together in a quiet discussion. When all five were seated, Michael was the one to reveal their decision.

"Well you men do not look the type to accept a pass, I am game, John your thoughts?"

John was motionless, he continued to stare down at the picture of Captain Leon Roger.

"John?" Michael repeated breaking John's deep concentration.

"Am I permitted to publish my own notes?" asked John.

The three men exchanged glances and without saying a word, William Rogers conferred their agreement with a nod.

"Your personal account would help to leverage public outcry by giving support to our charges against Leopold. Mr. Allen's permits will also be granted immediately upon your safe return," said Mr. Roberts

"Well gentlemen, it is settled then. Where do we go from here?" asked Michael.

"Mr. Meade has the papers for you to look over and sign. You will depart from Southampton by means of Royal Mail Service Dunbar which will take you to the port of Lagos. From there your liaison in Lagos will provide the manpower and equipment needed for your trek to Gerlache's compound in the Congo basin,' said Mr. Robert, 'Get home safely men."

"How are your sea legs my friend?" Michael asked with a cheery grin.

11

She could smell the oncoming approach. Carnivorous mammals, especially felines, have a very distinctive odor. Every animal in the jungle holds a definitive scent, reptiles though are the hardest to detect since their essence is camouflaged with the jungle's and can't be tracked until they are within direct range.

Jane Weaver crouched over her freshly killed gazelle preparing to use two pieces of rope to tie its legs together in order to transport it home. The sun was strong in the dry grasslands; there was no protection from the intense heat in the open land and soon, a famished scavenger would smell death and come scouting for its source.

Blood and death always attracted predators and despite her best efforts that is exactly what happened. Now, Jane found herself a short distance from her rifle and eye to eye with a very hungry female lion. Just a short distance away is enough to kill and with the hungry hunter positioned strategically on an overlooking boulder, Jane knew there were not many options at hand.

The beast watched methodically, switching its starving gaze from the gazelle to Jane.

Her father would have been greatly disappointed in her if he could see her now. It was a mistake leaving her rifle out of reach, he always taught her to treat one's surroundings with respect and leaving your weapon out of grasp was an act that could result in death.

The lioness took a few steps forward, Jane instantly placed her hand on the hilt of the knife resting in her belt. Straightening her legs into a partial crouching position so her body was directly over the dead gazelle to establish dominance and letting the opposing predator know that she would not be intimidated. The hungry female stepped off the edge of the boulder onto the dry dirt, moving within a few steps of striking distance.

Jane watched as the lioness prepared to take another step forward, she straightened her legs to a full stand, simultaneously removing her knife in a tight fist with the blade facing down for a better defensive strike. She stepped across the gazelle placing her right leg over the dead animal in a wide stance to fully cover her kill.

Jane could see the realization in the beast's eyes. The lioness understood this would not be an easy loot, it knew that a battle for the gazelle was inevitable and it would not leave unscathed. There was a choice to be made: fight with the women for the meat with the lioness winning; risk the possibility of being mortally wounded and too physically weak to return back to the den; or retreat.

They never broke eye contact, Jane began to perspire profusely. Feeling the weight of the intense heat, the protection of her brown, wide brimmed hat was useless with the sun's current position in the sky.

Despite the factors at hand Jane was prepared to outlast the resolve of the predator and secretly hoped that the famished female did not have the energy for a fight.

The lioness let out a soft moan of disappointment, sniffed the air and moved into a dried brush disappearing into the thicket. Jane remained in position for a long moment, with knife in hand, to make sure there wasn't an ambush waiting. She smelled the air then listened and when the area felt secure she continued with her task.

She knelt down finishing her knot on the kill. When the ropes were secure she stepped to her backpack placed next to her gun and took out a canteen gulping down two long swallows of water. Jane Weaver replaced the canteen, put on her backpack, picked up her rifle and surveyed the area. She walked back to the gazelle grabbing the ropes and began dragging her kill through the dry plane.

Jane moved promptly, doing her best not to make extensive noise, keeping both eyes on every bush and high grass that may be hiding any more oncoming scavengers.

Her eyes and ears kept track of her surroundings as she approached the end of the rocky, dehydrated grassland and the boundary edge of thick densely covered forest.

Stopping short at the edge of the forest, she smelled the air at the jungle opening searching for any irregularities then turned and looked to scan over the open range she had just covered.

Straightening up she released the grip she had on the ropes of the tied gazelle in order to check her rifle. After a moment of resting her arm she grabbed the rope moving forward into the dark rich flora confidently navigating through the hidden path she had traveled many times before.

Her home was deep in the thicket of jungle near a large rocky hill, well concealed from anyone attempting to follow.

At first appearance it would look like a group of boulders mixed with some bushes and an elephant graveyard. A closer examination would reveal the opening to the domicile of a skilled huntress.

Large bones from a dead elephant were used to extend the cave entrance creating a half tent over its opening. The inside of the tent was held up by elephant ribs set into the ground as reinforcement, a thick leather canvass covering the braces and various types of elephant bones created the walls on the outside cemented into place with dry clay.

The tent's opening was covered by a dried leather flap. There was a hole in the ceiling directly above a crater dug into the ground which was used as a fire pit.

The concealed entrance to the cave was directly opposite the entrance to the tent. The cavern was deeper than it was wide, a majority of the floor was carpeted with various animal pelts. Natural rock shelves on the sides held clay pots, tribal sculptures of various figures and two small unlit lamps.

In the right rear corner of the cave was a bed made with the stitched hides of leopards, cheetahs and lions packed with an assortment of dried grasses and leaves.

On the floor extending from her bed to the wall was the thick skin of a snake, different types of hunting and filleting knives displayed out on it. Next to the assortment of knives was a medium sized rifle, a large elephant gun, bags of gun powder and bullets as well as two hand revolvers. Behind the bedding on a natural rock ledge was a very large crocodile skull.

Jane walked up to the opening of the bone tent and let go of the gazelle. She dropped her pack in the bone tent and lit the fire, placing two pots of water on the burning wood.

She took her rifle into the cave and lit both of the lamps on the rock ledge, removing her hat and jacket she threw them into the left corner of the cave. Jane went to the end of her bedroom placing her rifle next to the others. She removed her hunting knife from her belt and placed it among the others, then grabbed a fillet knife and a large serrated edged blade putting them in her belt along with one of the handguns and turned to leave.

With the revolver and two knives in her belt and wearing just a hemp shirt, Jane grabbed two metal buckets from inside the bone tent and brought them outside next to the gazelle.

Jane walked with buckets in hand a short distance into the forest towards a clearing around a large tree. There were three wild dogs fighting over a large bone and sniffing the surrounding area. Standing at the edge of the clearing she quietly placed the buckets on the ground, removed her handgun and fired two close shots in the dirt near the dogs. The blast echoed in the forest startling the dogs which yipped and howled into the black jungle. She purposely shot close enough to scare them in order to deter them from returning any time soon but did not want to hurt them. A wounded dog would be ripped apart by its own kind and to leave an animal to that fate would have been a vicious act without any purpose except cruelty.

Jane set the buckets next to the tree near the center of the clearing and walked back to the bone tent retrieving the gazelle. A large rope was hung over a high branch of the tree with a hood at its end that sat limp in the dirt, the other end of the rope was fed into a winch which was nailed into the tree's base.

Jane brought the gazelle to the hook, placing it under the rope tying together the rear legs of the animal. She went over to the winch and cranked its lever raising the gazelle. When the beast's head was a little more than half her height off the ground, she clicked the hold to keep it in place.

Jane removed the serrated knife from her belt and slid the edge across the gazelle's neck spilling blood on the jungle floor.

She continued to cut off the beast's fur and to place the pieces into one of the buckets. Jane would later boil and make these into thick leather used as patch work for her clothing.

Jane then removed the organs and muscle, putting them into the other bucket. As she cut off each part, she mentally catalogued them into the good parts she would sell at the market or to traveling caravans and the lower quality cuts that she would keep for herself.

She would cook and salt some of the meat making nutritious meals for the next two days. Jane didn't care for gazelle meat or mammal meat for that matter, her father had raised her on reptile flesh believing that it made you stronger, it was a custom of old tribes located by deep rivers.

"The snakes and crocodiles have been here long before we ever emerged from Africa's womb. They will be here long after she decides we are done. We must utilize them for our own strength, but respect the meat for it is sacred. It is all a part of the codex," said Haggard Weaver.

There was a codex among the hunters who called Africa their home. Europeans, and Western travelers could never understand nor appreciate this and for that ignorance Mother Africa sometimes took them for examples.

Greed created an imbalance. For this Mother Africa, took retribution that could be felt all over the continent. She had seen this retribution many times on chartered trips with her father. Some of her fondest memories were of these expeditions with her father.

Tribal leaders would seek help with problems arising from this imbalance. It was said throughout many villages that only the infamous Haggard Weaver could bring back the balance when all other means proved insufficient.

Her father never liked to talk about these complimentary tales, and would shrug them off when other hunters would refer to him as "The Balance", but Jane understood that the trust and respect given to him by people of the land was due to his understanding and practice of the codex as well as his desire and love for Africa as a living breathing entity.

When she was very little her father taught her how to regard the codex properly as well as to respect the balance, teaching her the tribal customs and dialects of friendly villages, as well as which tribes to fear and avoid.

One of her earliest adventures and memories was travelling down a large river in a long boat, holding her first rifle. Haggard, facing her with his massive elephant gun, resting on his lap and three other men in the river boat along with them: two at the ends of the boat rowing and a shaman sitting in-between her and her father, chanting to ward off any water demons that might interfere with their task.

Haggard Weaver was explaining to her why they were on the river. Before she was born, one of the European Empires had moved into the region along the river and had killed an entire village. They had disposed of the bodies by throwing them into the water, before establishing their fated colony. A male crocodile began feeding off of the corpses and, without any rivals, grew to an immense size. For a decade he menaced the shores of the area forcing the Empire to abandon its colony and flee from the river. Another tribe further downstream lost many villagers especially the small children, greatly affecting their population. The leaders attempted to sacrifice animals to appease the river gods, but many children and fishermen continued to be killed or to go missing. The shaman spoke to the tribal council and recommend that it seek help from Haggard.

The fear in Jane's eyes as her father recounted this tale was obvious, she gripped her gun tighter pulling it higher up on her chest almost to her neck. The shaman had his back to her father, both men facing in her direction. She looked at her father who was occupied with intense focus scanning the river, the shaman reached over and smeared a smooth stroke of blue paint across one of her cheeks creating a circular shape.

"Fear not little one, for you are the daughter of Weaver. As long as you are embraced in the bosom of Africa she will not allow harm to come to you."

Jane never forgot that, the words swelling the confidence in her, something her father had always preached but never fully explained how to achieve.

In the boat there and then she realized confidence was not something to be taken but rather to be aroused from within. It came from the soul, the knowledge that you have control and are the one to take fate into your own hands.

They did not find Aca: The Great Snake, as it was known by the villagers. After a month the people decided that he must have been eaten by the river. It was believed that the flight of the European man, but more importantly, the presence of Haggard brought back the balance.

Her father was not so sure and promised them that if Aca did return, he would come back. Weeks later the entire tribe was attacked and killed by rivals hired and armed by another invading Empire. After the interloper built their colony and established their means of production, Aca returned and fed off of the river's edge again. Jane and Haggard heard of this when bartering with a caravan which was traveling through the western region they were exploring.

"Are we to return to help?" asked Jane.

"It is the way of the Mother. She always has a plan and we are to understand, it is not within our reach. We were not meant to interfere with Aca and must respect Africa's decision. We must not get in the way," he replied.

After a time, the tales of Aca and the Empire began to subside, Jane and Haggard kept their distance from that region along the river.

- - - -

After she finished removing the major portions of meat, all that remained were the legs connected to the spine, ribs and the head with horns. She clicked the winch releasing the remains to crash to the ground.

Jane walked over to the carcass, grabbed one of the horns, and with one quick chop of her knife cut the skull free from the neck. She thought about cleaning it and bringing it with her to one of the colonys or river cities to trade, it wouldn't be worth much but if she found a novice traveler, she would be able to negotiate an inflated price for it.

The traveler could bring it back to his country of origin as a present to one of his children or as office decor, telling an inflated tale of courage and danger.

As Jane pondered, she heard movement in the darkness of the jungle and instantly smelled the wild dogs pacing back and forth, admiring her freshly cut pieces of meat and yearning for the cleaved remains at her feet.

She threw the head into the darkness and saw the shadows of their bodies follow, and heard the aggressive snarls and howls for the battle over the gazelle's head. Jane grabbed both buckets and headed back to her home leaving behind the remains of the body for the dogs to fight over. If they were smart, they would control their aggression and share the head and carcass before a larger predator came through to steal it from them.

When she returned to the bone tent both pots of water were boiling. Jane placed the pieces of skin one at a time into one of the pots. She unwrapped a large piece of leather next to the bucket, going through the meat and organs, separating what she would keep for herself and what she would bring to the market the next day. Jane grabbed a small bag of salt from one of the corners of the tent and sprinkled palm sized amounts over all the pieces making sure not to over salt but just enough to preserve the juices to last the night and her long trek to the market the following day.

Jane removed a piece of cloth from her pocket and prepared to clean her knife of the blood and pieces of flesh that caked on it. She dipped the knife in the boiling water, removed it then wiped it clean with the piece of cloth.

She grabbed the piece of meat she had set aside for herself and cooked it over the fire. Pulling off chunks of charred flesh, still dripping with inner juice and blood, she thought about how much she disliked mammal meat, it reminded her of cannibalistic tribes that fed off of the flesh of war captives. She reflected on the remains of the gazelle being ripped apart by a pack of vicious wild dogs, a similarity to cannibals savagely feeding off of the burnt flesh of those they defeated in battle, in order to consume their strength.

She considered adventure seekers from the outer Empires stepping onto the continent. If only they were fully aware of the horrors and deadly challenges that lay facing them in the unknown. Many hunters of her caliber profited handsomely by taking these seekers on group excursions into parts of the jungle to hunt the famed exotic beasts of the dark continent. Most of the time the smarter ones would take the European and even American adventurers into regions that posed no threat. They would coax animals into the open to set up decent shots for the paying explorers and many times these rich men would bag themselves a sick lion or an injured giraffe for their cigar room or office back in their "civilized" land.

The greedier hunters were fully aware of what lay in the vast dark regions of Africa and would take parties into the uncharted regions, promising gems and riches as well as dangerous beasts that no man had ever seen. Often these unknowing groups never returned or, those who did, would go straight onto a boat at port retreating to their native land, never to speak of Africa again.

The talk was always the same: stories of old gods taking them as sacrifices for trespassing violations, attempting to pillage the forbidden treasurers of Africa. Some, mad with fear, would claim they saw the forest come alive and ravage their party.

Her hunter brethren would wave off these stories as African Tales but Jane Weaver knew better, she had seen the old gods and what they could do. One of these jungle demons had taken her father, leaving a scarred impression on her for the remainder of her life.

Jane was trained as she became a woman, with a mind matured beyond her years, Haggard began entrusting Jane with her own charters and contracts to venture out to lead expeditions that he would normally lead himself.

That faithful day they were approached by a British military man in a city off the Nile. The Commander was looking for a regiment of soldiers who were missing from their base and who were possibly dead. He explained to Haggard that a few of his men had heard a story of a mine in French West Africa that possibly had an endless supply of diamonds and that they purchased a map from a known opium dealer in the area. The Commander had a replica of the map of the mine that he "coerced" from the dealer which he handed to Haggard. He said heard the stories of the infamous Haggard Weaver, from the central African plane all the way to the Queen's territories and needed his assistance in locating his missing soldiers.

Haggard studied the map and handed it to Jane, she looked it over then folded it up and put it into her pocket. The Commander looked at Jane then looked at her father who explained that he would make no promises, but reassured the Commander that they would be in contact in a month's time with the status of his soldiers.

The Commander attempted to give Haggard payment but he refused and said payment would be accepted when they had information. When they left the bar and were on the way back to meet up with their caravan for the journey home Haggard read Jane's thoughts.

"These are the type of men you do not want to be indebted to," he said.

Her father did not trust the European or American colonists, he believed that their word was a symbol of intended deception, a quick sale to get what they wanted and later choose if they would honor an agreement if or when it suited their purposes.

What Haggard Weaver disliked the most was the misogynistic structure of their social policies. He believed that their treatment of women was comparable to their treatment of animals: kept as ornamental household amenities which was a display of their inferiority.

Even the so called "savage" societies in the tribal planes showed respect to their women and some even worshiped them as deities. The reason that Africa was called "Mother" was because it can create life. He liked to believe that he had raised Jane in the exact same way he would have raised a son, teaching her the survival skill necessary for the day when he would no longer be with her.

As a woman it was obvious that the courtesies which were afforded her father, were not necessarily afforded to Jane.

She often attracted unwanted attention from men in the cities who were not familiar with women of the jungle.

The previous night, at the same bar, a cargo trader between ports attempted to grab Jane when she was waiting for the drinks she was buying for her father and an Englishman in a suit who were discussing the possibility of work in exchange for goods.

Jane with her back to the man in rapid response unsheathed her hunting blade and without the man being aware, moved it blade side up between his legs. The man immediately dropped to his knees screaming, with blood covering his legs, pooling around his knees. The barkeep put her three drinks on the bar paying no attention to the screaming man and Jane dropped two pieces of silver on the counter.

"For the mess," she said to the bartender.

She grabbed the drinks and turned around heading back to the table without the slightest bit of acknowledgement to the man, on the floor, holding his groin.

The businessman was speechless. Few whispers and inaudible comments were exchanged but, other than that, conversations around them continued uninterrupted. The injured assailant was picked up off the floor and brought outside. No one addressed Jane about the incident and Haggard never once flinched or showed concern.

Haggard on his own had stature and of course his daughter was recognized as well, for those familiar with the two it was obvious that the man had it coming.

After a week of traveling south with a caravan they traded for supplies and then parted ways with the traveling nomads.

The two had an extra day and half back to their home, Jane and Haggard spent a full day at their camp preparing for the search and discussing the best possible route to intercept the group which already had a few weeks head start. Both were fully aware that the possibility of the soldiers being alive was slim and the necessity to press for time was of no importance especially since her father was already suspicious of this mission.

After a full three days journey into the thick jungle they picked up the tracks of inexperienced travelers wearing military style boots. Their heavy steps and the broken path left behind showed they had no previous knowledge of the area or that there wasn't an attempt to cover their course. Following the tracks for half a day Jane realized that they were stopping every few meters or so, there was a pattern that showed they were probably lost and most likely checking on the map for directions.

"They are too easy to track," Jane said in a hushed tone.

She was cautious for the fact that if they had such an easy time following the group of men then less friendly individuals would have just as easy a time. The number of prints told them there were six men. As Haggard and Jane followed them around large hills and crevices in the ground, it became clear that they were seriously off-course and were not too far ahead.

"They keep retracing their steps and second guessing the direction they are going," Jane said.

She was kneeling in the dirt looking at the crisscrossed prints and scrutinizing the smell in the air for any hint of proximity.

"We could come upon their bones within a day or two," Haggard answered.

She understood his reasoning. There was a tribe, ruled by a class of matriarchs, over a small rise of mountains from where the map was directing them. These women were known to consume the flesh of men following ritualistic acts of procreation. It was uncommon for the tribe to move this far but a group of loud men blindly following a hopeless trail could draw them out of their perimeter especially if they were strongly built and the tribe thought the men would father strong children.

Jane at first thought that the soldiers were sold a foolish map, a desperate opium dealer's idea to lead them off into dangerous territory hoping that they would never return. The city areas were riddled with opium dens and havens for illicit behavior that altered the mind. Desperation did not prevent a man from sending another to his doom even for the smallest of price.

They heard falling water and correctly assumed that the men would go to a source of a natural spring. Stepping into a clearing they found a waterfall with a large pool at the base. There must have been a deep cavern behind the fall, due to the current flowing under the falling water, and there was no outlet for the pool. The consistent size regardless of the immense amount of water flowing into it meant that the water from the fall had to be going into an underground area.

In the pool there were three bodies floating on their stomachs, the heads had been removed at the neck and their military attire was similar to that of the Commander's.

The bodies showed signs of having been there for a few days; there was little blood in the pool and the bodies were bloated from soaking in the water. Jane could see that some of the creatures living in the water gradually fed on the open hole of the neck and on chunks of flesh missing from the water logged hands.

A large rock came sailing down at them from over the falls, landing directly behind Jane and Haggard. Unable to see who threw it, from where they stood, Jane and Haggard instantly ducked raising their guns and ran into the forest at opposite sides.

Jane hooked right of the falls and Haggard moved to the left, both understanding the course of action was to get toward the top to discover their attacker.

The situation was curious and was full of mystery, armed soldiers would not revert to throwing rocks. If the women of the tribe had discovered the group, why would the huntress only take the heads and waste the rest of the meat from the bodies?

Moving up the hill with the falls to her left, the sound of the forest was drowned out by the loud crashing of water into the pool below, the remainder of her senses were on heightened alert awaiting any movement or a change in her surroundings. Halfway to the top, the hill got steeper and it took time to proceed with stealth. Jane positioned her gun pointing to the highest spot for any aggression that might come from the high ground. Her real concern was for Haggard. Jane felt a rush of anxiety and the urgent need to ignore what he had taught her about moving towards danger and to proceed as quickly as she could.

For the first time in her life, thoughts circulated in her head that he was in danger, but she refused to let her guard down. Jane attempted to increase the stride of her steps without making novice mistakes, if her father were in danger then it would be foolish to give up her own position and allow whoever lurked at the top of the falls to get the best of her.

Jane reached the river bend at the top of the hill flowing into the falls. Her father was on the opposite side of the bulging river, fighting off what looked like four grey chimpanzees. The beasts were no bigger than an adolescent child, they had grey torsos and white stripes of hair on their backs. She could see even from her distance that their faces were disfigured, teeth were broken in fractured shards, faces plagued with large grey boils that protruded all over their heads disfiguring their appearance.

Jane knew that she was looking at the legendary Ufiti, Ghost Apes that hunt men and protect sacred mines of long dead masters and old gods.

Ghost Apes or not, Jane was not going to let her father be taken. Haggard was able to get his knife out and stabbed one in the side, it howled off of him landing on the ground. She shot the beast directly in the head as it prepared for another leaping attack with blood poring out from under its arm.

The top of its skull blew off into pieces and the grey hair on its shoulders stained red, the corpse of the Ufiti collapsed to the ground. The echoing reverberation from her gun did nothing to deter the others from their quest to lay siege on her father.

Jane moved knee deep into the water for a closer shot and fired off two more rounds, hitting one directly in the chest and another in head. The one she hit in the chest lay on its stomach and attempted to get back up but instantly fell face down into the dirt, a pool of blood formed underneath it. Jane began to reload her rifle calling out to her father to come across the river when the one remaining Ufiti slammed its arms on the ground and let out a primordial roar, it was a sound she never heard an ape make and it froze her.

Haggard Weaver attempted to run over to the edge of the forest where his rifle lay, a large hairy hand grabbed it, picked it up and tossed the gun over the waterfall. An Ufiti taller than Haggard stepped out of the dark jungle towards him. Its face was full of the grotesque boils, the creature did not appear to have eyes just large black empty holes sunk into the irregularly raised flesh. Haggard was stunned in position holding his blood caked knife in front of him.

The remaining Ufiti fell to its knees and extended its arms to the ground lowering its head as if it were praying. The great monster swiped an open palmed assault into her father's head, Haggard collapsed to the ground on his back with a large gaping wound bleeding out from the crown of his skull.

Jane rapidly tried to finish reloading but was caught in the dream like nature of the situation. Before she could finish entering the next round of bullets into her rifle, the beast stood over her father's unconscious body and smashed its massive fist directly through his rib cage grabbing his heart from the exposed cavity. Blood exploded all over the arm of the Ufiti. The monster raised its clenched fist out of her father's lifeless body, holding the remaining pieces of Haggard's heart, and licking the fist of bloody meat. The Ufiti turned its head and looked directly at Jane, she released a loud roar of anger, raised her rifle and fired two shots dead on at the Ufiti.

The leaves of the forest behind the monster tore apart from the blast of her bullets, they appeared to move directly through their intended target. The monster turned its body and retreated into the forest with the other Ufiti following behind. Both creatures completely disappearing into the darkness as if they never existed.

Jane ran across the river, its deepest part rising to her waist. Reaching the other shore, she stood over her father's corpse with her gun raised staring directly into the black forest, scanning for the remnants of the wraith she just witnessed. The forest lay quiet and she stood there silently protecting his body like a stone sentinel. After a while a creeping hyena entered from the shadows, leaving the forest it stepped towards Jane raised its nose smelling the air and then ran back from whence it came.

That night Haggard Weaver's body was cremated according to the customs of his favorite tribe. They performed a ritualistic chant of the dead and painted him with symbols they used for transitioning the body back with the land.

Jane sat a short distance from the pyre, crying on a stone, watching his body burn. Her tears silently rolled down her face mutely cursing the old gods and their vile children.

The top religious shaman stepped away from the encircling chanters and walked towards her, bending down he offered her his pipe. She took a drag holding the smoke to sooth her emotions and to calm her mind.

"He is with Mistress Earth now little one," he said to her with his soft voice, "weep for his absence, but do not weep for his soul for he is one now with the energy of the land."

She did not say anything in reply, releasing the smoke, she never moved her eyes off of the fire.

"Remember that you are Jane Weaver. You are important to Mistress Earth, mother of Africa. Holding us all on her back, she needs you now more than ever."

Jane took another drag of the pipe then handed it back to him, tears still dripping down her face.

"The mother will never let any harm come to you. Your fate is a part of her soil."

He let her be and walked back over to the chanters.

Jane watched as he took a pull from his pipe and blew the smoke into the burning face of Haggard, repeating a sacred chant.

She felt very much alone and on her own now, still young in age Jane felt a surge of fear but pushed it back ignoring the feeling. The dark continent felt much darker to her at that moment than it ever had.

As the night proceeded and the ritual finished her father's body was reduced to ash. Tribal elders and warriors emerged from beyond the shadows around the smoldering embers, these were not the members of the local tribe but travelers from great distances who had come to pay respects. Each elder and warrior alike came over to the ash and chanted a single prayer bending down grabbing a handful of grey powdery remains smearing it across their chests over their hearts. After each did this they would step back and allow other members to take their turn until there was a large group surrounding the spent fire, illuminated by fixed torches. They began to chant together a single phrase, Jane saw that they were no longer staring at the spent pyre but at her, all together chanting: "Mistress Earth."

III

John stood port side looking over the calm ocean. Land appeared on the horizon, signaling the ship's approach into the Gulf of Guinea. He enjoyed the past twenty-two days on the Dunbar, entertaining himself in the mid-level accommodations reserved for first class passengers. Michael, on the other hand, spent a majority of the time heaving the contents of his stomach overboard, or in the waste room connected to their shared lodging. Only a few hours after departing from Southampton, Michael discovered he did not have the greatest sea legs, his stomach unfortunately absorbing most of the discomfort.

There was a doctor onboard who provided Michael with a tonic that helped him through some of the most trying moments, but the doctor and John shared a fearful concern that any prolonged delay in their voyage would put his friend's health in serious jeopardy.

Back in England when the two men arrived at Castle Port in Southampton they stood in awe and marveled at the R.M.S. Dunbar. A little over a hundred and twenty meters with two sail masts and double exhaust funnels, she was a newer model of a twin-screw propeller with a maximum speed advertised at 14 knots. The estimated arrival time to the Gulf of Guinea was twenty-five days, but now, staring over the beautiful water and the jungle horizon getting closer it appeared they would be entering harbor almost two days ahead of schedule.

Lagos was originally a fishing community that grew into a larger commerce center for British trade. An extensive portion of its exports were rare oils harvested from various palms and plants along the Niger river that ran west of the vastly growing community.

As they entered the harbor, making their way into the Lagoon of Lagos, John was taken aback by the size of the colony's port. His sheer excitement urged him to run off of the ship and to see every end of Lagos. This impatience had John anxiously pacing from bow to stern, quickening his stride as the ship closed in on the land.

When they were secured to the dock the crew aided by workers on land began to unload the cargo. John quickly ran down the wooden gangway onto the pier almost losing his footing and falling into the water below. Stepping onto the planked pier he was finally able to calm himself by looking out over the lagoon which was lined with exotic trees, groups of buildings standing proudly behind them.

Lagos sounded like any major English city, but John had to remind himself that he was new here. This was a foreign land far from the safety of his London streets, he was the stranger and should tread lightly.

"Sir, I think you forgot your companion," called a voice from behind him.

He turned to face a member of the ship's crew aiding a visibly weak Michael, making their way down the gangway.

John ran up to help the man assist Michael down to the landing of the pier. He locked arms under his friend's and turned his head, locking eyes for a quick moment with Michael, forcing himself to make an uncomfortable smile. At first John thought Michael was going to make his customary quip, but before he was able to speak, he was quickly overcome with a fit of gagging, fell to his knees, and threw up over the edge of the pier into the water. John looked down thinking he should possibly assist but pushed against this idea allowing Michael a little more time to adjust being back on land.

He thought that while he awaited Michael's return to normalcy, he should arrange for the logistical move of their luggage, then locate their contact here in Lagos.

A man wearing tan khakis, a white cotton shirt, and recently shined brown dress shoes, walked directly up to him. John couldn't help but appreciate the man's well-groomed mustache and welcoming familiar face.

"Mr. Alpert I presume?"

John was stunned for a moment, not by how nicely this African man was dressed but how proper his English accent was.

"Yes I am," said John.

"I am Monroe Kelly, your contact here. Welcome to Lagos."

"Your accent?" John asked immediately embarrassed feeling his question was rude and too forward.

"My birth parents were killed during a conflict in the eastern region. My adoptive parents were missionaries. I had the privileged of being schooled on Her Majestys soil before they moved us back to Africa to spread the good word," replied Monroe.

"How rude of me... I must apologize Mr. Kelly. John Alpert, and this fellow at my feet is my friend and business partner Michael Allen," John said putting his hand out for a customary shake.

"The sea is not for everyone. I have a carriage ready. We will put your bags in the back and if you do not mind sitting in the front, we could spread Mr. Allen down in the coach seats so he may get some rest."

"That would be splendid. I would like to express my gratitude Mr. Kelly," said John.

"If it pleases you call me Monroe. I have a nice stogie for the both of us as we make our way to the building where you will be staying."

John shook his head in agreement, it pleased him greatly to be greeted by a warm face and familiar voice. He was ashamed to admit it but hearing an English accent made him less melancholy at being so far from home. Monroe assisted John in lifting Michael into the back seat of their carriage and then coordinated the crew from the boat to move their belongings on to their transport.

The carriage took them through the colony's center. As they traveled, Monroe described the history of Lagos. He briefly explained the annexation, 30 years prior, and the creation of a liberated African yard which gave freed slaves employment opportunities and rights under British law.

"You are a British citizen?" asked John.

"Not precisely. There are two types of African citizens in Lagos-those who are born here are considered protected by British common law; those born outside of the city are under jurisdiction of their traditional rulers. My parents' appropriation of me at infancy granted me the same rights of those born in Lagos, but I am not considered a British citizen. Many Africans here do not care for my inherent rights," he said taking a puff of his cigar never allowing his eyes to stray from the flat dirt path ahead of them.

"I was led to believe Lagos was a failed colony due to the outside forces that threatened it," said John.

"It was considered to be failed due to the war between the Abeokuta and the Ibadan. That aggression was calmed and our

Governor, Captain Maloney, has assured Parliament that the Abeokuta pose no danger. Due to lack of resources they have been unable to successfully attack our presence in the lagoon," Monroe explained.

"Is there fear from retaliation of freed Africans?"

"This is a haven Mr. Alpert. That type of aggression would not be beneficial to anyone and would only lead to more bloodshed. Africa has seen too much blood spilled already," replied Monroe.

"I hope you do not find my prying disagreeable," John said taking a great interest in the buildings they passed and the people moving about them. He was amazed by the busy commerce at work, making the flourishing colony operate.

"None the sort Mr. Alpert. If you do not object, I hope to inquire into your forthcoming meeting with Jonkheer Gerlache," Monroe said looking at John.

"Jonkheer?"

"Gerlache prefers to go by Jonkheer. An honorary title bestowed upon him by the King of Belgium," explained Monroe.

"Please Monroe call me John. This information is most valuable. Anything else you think we should know, that could be beneficial in completing our task, would be greatly appreciated," said John.

"You and your friend are to meet with the most unsavory of characters. I am aware there is a political maneuver behind your visit, which could be very dangerous if not carefully calculated. What have you decided upon as a cover story?" Monroe pressed.

"I have not thought about it yet. I understand that there is an account here in Lagos, under the name of our ringer company, that would be helpful with the front," John replied with a nervous tone.

During his weeks at sea he never once considered what he was going to say when introduced to Gerlache. Perhaps he should have been more invested in the research and due diligence behind his current mission, instead of being caught up in the moment at sea. He suddenly felt like he was standing in front of one of his editors expecting a story, when he had yet to write a single word.

"The fund here in Lagos backs the financial cover, but if I may interject a recommendation?" said Monroe as he tapped the end of his cigar knocking off the thick ash.

"Please, I insist," John replied.

"Mr. Allen...Michael is the business intellect when it comes to this fictitious arrangement. His can be accounted for by experience. You, on the other hand, do not possess the intricate knowledge that he does. Your participation could be dismantled if put under scrutiny," explained Monroe.

Another troubling factor, John thought, was that this had not crossed his mind either. The idea of improvising the meeting had been his original plan which was obviously flawed. Monroe was correct that if John was pressed, his ruse may crack and he would be exposed, putting himself and Michael in serious danger.

"I take it Monroe you have considered what I regrettably have not. What do you have in mind?" asked John.

"I would propose you position yourself as Mr. Allen's book-keeper. His numbers man, to verify that the figures are beneficial to the company. That way your presence as well as any notes taken or information collected while in the compound will not raise suspicion."

"That is brilliant. Any rational business man would travel with his accountant when negotiating a large deal," John said, the statement was more a commentary to himself than a reply to Monroe.

"Precisely," Monroe answered looking at John with a smirk.

They sat in silence enjoying the cigars in hand, John couldn't help but be amazed by his surroundings. It was not quite as John imagined an African colony would be. Lagos was similar to an English hamlet but with strange foliage and even stranger architecture. He couldn't point to a style that even remotely suggested English influence, but there was a dominate design that was unfamiliar to John.

"How many people live in Lagos?" asked John.

"Fifty Thousand, less than 400 derive from the Commonwealth."

The carriage pulled in front of a beautiful two storied building with wraparound terraces on both floors. All windows were open giving John comfort in the thought that his room would not be as stifling hot as the outside.

Monroe spoke Afrikan to the porters out front who immediately grabbed their bags, bringing them inside. Both men lifted Michael out of the back of the carriage, they walked in through the front entrance and carried him up the central staircase. Monroe directed John down the short hall to their adjoining rooms.

The rooms were already open with their luggage placed in the corner. Monroe and John laid a frail Michael on the bed.

He looked around the room examining its small size. There was a writing desk against one wall and a nightstand next to the bed. The double doors at the back wall were wide open leading to the shared balcony.

"I will be leaving you to make arrangements for our caravan to the compound. Then I will telegraph the home station of your timely arrival. If it pleases you, we will meet downstairs in a few hours for some spirits then discuss how the following days will play out," Monroe explained.

"Sounds excellent, Monroe."

"Your room is next door, here are the keys," he said placing two sets on the desk.

"There is stationary available downstairs at the front desk if you would like to pen a letter. I would recommend doing so before we depart. The Royal Mail Service leaves for Britain in a few weeks and you will not get another chance to send mail until we return from Gerlache's compound."

"I am grateful, Monroe, for all your assistance," said John.

Monroe nodded then turned and left the room. John walked out through the open doors and stood on the balcony gripping the top of the railing. He looked over the city and the magnificent mountain ranges that stretched out far into the depths of the horizon. John could not imagine what was hidden under the sheet of forest thinking, with a small stretch of his imagination, what fantastic and mystical splendors it held. Looking at the vast stretch of forest and contemplating the impact of travel in days to come, he held a small doubt.

'In less than 3 days we are to dive head first into the bosom of Africa. Are we prepared for such a journey?' he thought.

When Michael finally arose, they decided to go down to the common area for drinks and food. Both men were seated instantly into their own area with a table surrounded by three chairs and a day sofa.

John looked around and was reminded of an English library except, in place of books, the walls were decorated with oil paintings of heroic hunters and busts of various exotic beasts such as lions and zebras. He could see the head of an amazing elephant on the far wall across the dining area.

They ordered a meat and coconut milk dish. John wondered what animal the meat had come from but when he asked the servant, the man did not understand, he just smiled with a slight bow, and walked away. Michael said it was probably for the best, that he was unlikely to enjoy the meal if he knew where it came from.

There was a bar nearby. Michael stood up and said he was sure he heard the bartender speaking English. He excused himself, heading towards the bar wanting some type of tonic to wash down the strange flavor of the food and to calm his raw stomach.

While he was gone Monroe entered the area immediately making eye contact with John. He was wearing a different set of khaki pants and an open collared white shirt. John assumed this was the standard attire for the African weather and made a mental note to add these garments to their wardrobes.

As Monroe made his way towards their table, John could hear snarky whispers, accompanied by astounded glares, from some of the patrons in the room. Monroe sat opposite John on the day couch and removed his hat.

"Is there something amiss I am not aware of?" asked John.

"I am African," Monroe said matter-of-factly.

"These are not free lands under Her Majesty's Flag?" John asked.

"Free does not always mean free, there are always stipulations. This is considered a white man's establishment," said Monroe.

"Shall we continue our business elsewhere?" asked John.

"I am a naturalized citizen of Lagos with business on behalf of Britain. If people are uncomfortable, they can move. I will not," Monroe stated proudly.

As he was saying this Michael approached the area placing two glasses on the table. He looked at Monroe and smiled, obviously back to his normal self with his usual energy and excitement.

"Mr. Kelly! I am very appreciative of your assistance while I was incapacitated," Michael said, sitting down then extending his hand for Monroe to shake.

"Please...call me Monroe."

"I must apologize for not getting you a drink. What will you be having?" ask Michael.

"Thank you, Mr. Allen, I am quite alright," answered Monroe.

Monroe took out a small cigar lighting it as he sat back against the couch, crossing his legs. He looked relaxed despite the awkward feeling brought on by casual glances of disgust offered by random diners.

"Have you and John discussed the meeting with Jonkheer Gerlache?" asked Monroe exhaling a cloud of smoke.

"We discussed it briefly and consider your idea the best course of action. However, I thought the mock transaction was for the exchange of rubber trees. Are we altering it to the procurement of slaves?" Michael asked with a bit of discomfort.

"That is correct. You see the mission, as I have been briefed, is to gain knowledge about the slave trafficking in the region. Rubber trading would not suffice for us in gaining the information we need," Monroe elaborated.

"Under Secretary Roberts felt that the rubber tree deal was a sufficient ruse," Michael replied.

"Gerlache has seen some trouble with many of his fields and rubber would be an option but my sources tell me his profits are not hurting," Monroe said taking a puff of his small cigar

"Slaves are the key to Jonkheer Gerlache's appetite. A direct invitation to his table through that means would give the best opportunity for a peek into his operations. The pact in Berlin has left the supply of slave labor dwindling. If he finds an option to gain a slave source from another region it would be too tempting for a man like Gerlache to refuse."

John and Michael sat in silent consent. It was clear on their faces they did not savor the idea of posing as slave traders, but knew their lives were in the hands of Monroe's knowledge and trusted the man on his expertise.

"The true danger is not Jonkheer. The man is a spoiled Belgian dignitary, easily moved by compliments and expensive gifts. His man and confidant, Captain Leon Roger, is the true predator. We will need to be on point around him, he will pry apart any weakness in our story. Jonkheer pays him well enough to expose potential enemies and threats to his enterprise," said Monroe.

"We are his enemy?" stuttered John.

"You are going into his home under false pretenses to extract information for an opposing nation. I would not consider that to be the act of a friend but an adversary. Under no circumstances are you to forget that he is yours as well. This is Africa, never let your guard down or it will kill you."

Monroe went into detail of what they should expect when they arrived at the grounds of Gaston Gerlache. This meeting was to be a brainstorming session but turned into a full lesson for accomplishing their mission with success. It became clear to both John and Michael that they were in over their heads. They were grateful they had a man like Monroe Kelly guiding their way.

Monroe explained that he would be recruiting five men to assist them on their journey. He would change his accent and speak in Afrikan dialect, using limited English while in the presence of these men and during their time in the compound.

Michael went to get John and himself another set of drinks. As he returned Monroe was almost finished with his cigar, when a man in a white jacket approached the table and asked Monroe to leave.

John was about to stand and protest when Monroe lightly grabbed his arm and pulled him back down to his seat.

"That is quite alright gents, I feel we have concluded our business for the day. Let us meet at the clock tower after breakfast tomorrow and I will introduce you to the team," Monroe said unfazed.

They all stood, exchanging handshakes, Monroe then picked up his hat looking eye to eye with the employee of the lodging, then dropped the stub of his cigar on the floor.

John watched with astonishment and admiration as Monroe confidently put on his hat and strolled back out through the doors to the streets of Lagos.

Later that night, alone in his room, John contemplated that Monroe was the true agent at work, he and Michael were only figureheads to help Monroe infiltrate Gerlache's operation.

He penned his sister a note writing of Lagos and their time at sea, leaving out the part about Michael's weak stomach. He explained that they would be departing for their twelve-day journey into the Congo Free State in two days' time and would be out of contact until they returned. John attempted to tell Margaret how much he missed her company and that the time away had been difficult, but the words escaped his mind and his pen.

He sat on the bed looking over his letter, thinking of what to say. Rereading what he already written, the impact of the journey he began and what was before him weighed heavily on his mind.

It would be close to a month at sea and almost two weeks journey traveling through an unfamiliar jungle, followed by an undisclosed time in the Belgium region and that was not considering the journey back.

This would be the longest he had spent away from home. Even when he attended Cambridge, he would return every few weeks, but this was an extraordinary undertaking. He didn't even want to entertain the idea of any setbacks that may arise once they set off. The idea of an extended delay prolonging his return to England was unnerving. Whenever he attempted to think what possibly could go wrong, John felt a rising fear that he may never make it back. He gripped the letter with a desperation that this would be the last moment he had to speak to those he loved. John left his letter on the night stand next to the bed, then stood up abruptly heading over to the open doors of the balcony looking over Lagos. He saw the lit street lamps and random carts moving along the dirt road, trying to picture a visualize a comparison to London. As his thoughts drifted over the beautiful image of Lagos, he completely forgot about the letter he was writing. He closed his eyes absorbing the cool night air and listening to the sounds of the jungle birds in the distance. It calmed him, returning the send of confidence he had felt the moment he stepped of the boat onto this foreign land,

He turned back into the room to prepare for sleep and for the days to come-his letter left unfinished on the dresser.

IV

The heat beating down through the trees was unbearable, sweat dripped from Mumba Nkusa's head making the grueling task at hand even more difficult than it already was. He dared not move to wipe the sweat away for fear that the men with guns would accuse him of lax behavior, resulting in a severe physical assault or maiming.

Mumba was his birth name, born in a village far from where he was now, men from another land with white skin gave him a different title. Though he would acknowledge it, he would never betray his family by giving up what was passed down from his grandfather to his father and then bestowed upon him.

He did not know the exact number of days since he had been with his wife and children, but it felt like an eternity. The last images he held were burnt into his mind, his wife being dragged off into the night screaming his name as he was thrown to the ground helpless to protect her.

The invaders slaughtered those who attempted to fight, grabbing the women by their hair, pulling them away from their crying young ones or even violating them right there for the children to see. The lucky ones were killed immediately without having to suffer the anguish of the living.

The night they came Mumba awoke to the noise of onslaught, he quickly aroused both his children and hurried his wife to the back of their home giving instructions for them all to run into the woods and not to stop.

The four of them made their escape to the outer most part of the village at the edge of forest before shots were fired, in their direction. Running hard his wife was thrown to the ground by a man on a horse from behind, his young daughter trampled, pounded by the steed's charging hooves. Mumba quickly stopped running and turned to see his daughter's lifeless body down in the dirt. He called her name uncaring of the imposing danger, his legs were struck hard forcing Mumba to the ground. The man on the horse yelling orders at the other men to drag his wife away, the attacker was unmoved that his bronco was on the lifeless body of a little girl.

After the screaming stopped and the dead were tossed into a pile, all the able-bodied men were lined up with their backs against the embers of their burning villager.

There were six white men on horseback wearing white uniforms, their numerous soldiers had red and blue uniforms but the same skin color as Mumba and his fellow villagers. They were told in their own language that they were now the property of a distant empire. They were to be given new names and a new place to live. Their families would be cared for only if they did as they were told, and not dare defy the men in uniform or great harm would come to them and their families.

Despite his broken ankle, Mumba was chained to another man; they were directed to cut down a large section of the forest and to burn what remained. His job was changed days later to work an expanse of trees. Mumba was told by a fellow slave that the white man valued the trees' blood.

Throughout the day, a man working with Mumba would take a knife cutting a deep laceration from the middle of the tree trunk down to the roots. White fluid would flow out and Mumba was told to place buckets at the base of each tree to collect the sticky white liquid flowing from these cuts. After these buckets filled, he was instructed to pore the liquid into a large funnel on a cart then repeat the process. One day when the pain in the poorly heeling ankle was extreme, Mumba tripped, spilling the bucket of liquid on the ground. A soldier, a white man called Charles came over to Mumba and began to berate him.

Charles pointed to the bucket and told Mumba that he would be working extra-long today to make up for the wasted liquid. Ordering Mumba to get up, Charles took a thick rod made with Rhinoceros tail and hit him on the back. Mumba held himself to the ground unable to control his cries of pain as the man hit him over and over again, opening large bleeding slashes on his back. When the man finally stopped, two other slaves Mumba knew from his village came to his aid and helped him onto his hobbled feet. They picked up the bucket, one of the men gave it to Mumba and assured Charles that they would help him make up for what he had lost.

The following day Mumba's back was excruciatingly painful, he attempted to work through it trying to double his efforts to make up for the bucket he had spilled the day before. Charles walked up to Mumba taking something out of a pouch at his side then tossed the objected at him. Mumba looked down unsure of what it was. Bending to pick it up, he was shocked to see he was holding the severed hand of a small child. Dropping it immediately he began to shake, Charles with a vile grin told Mumba that they had taken it off of his son and the next time it would be his wife's head. A group of other uniformed men gathered at a distance listening, all waiting for Mumba's reaction. Mumba humbled his rising anger, he bowed his head forcing a nod of understanding then turned his body to continue his work.

Throughout the day he tempered his emotions, pushing the image of his son, missing a hand, away from his thoughts. He wanted to believe it was not his son's and that they took the hand off of a corpse to illustrate their point, but his heart told him they were not lying and that these hellish men were full of repulsive truths.

Escape was a dangerous concept, even though the thought had entered his mind more than enough times, he considered it to be detrimental to his family's survival. Mumba once saw a man from his village run for the woods. The man was caught within minutes and they chopped both of his arms off at the elbows. Now he has a large shackle around his neck and pulls the wheeled device that collects the liquid.

A breeze moved through the crop of rubber trees, the cool air offering a moment of gratifying relief. Mumba was enjoying a moment of bliss from the wind when he noticed an unnatural hush in the forest around him.

The days were always filled with the sound of busy work, the men in uniform yelling at the slaves or even at each other, but there was always the background noise from the forest around them. Even the nights were filled with screeches of monkies and insects buzzing. The sudden muted atmosphere was not only noticed by Mumba but also by the men working alongside of him. Everyone, even the uniformed forces stopped to look around when the silence was immediately destroyed with a thunderous noise. Mumba thought of the cracking roar of Shango, God of Thunder breaking the ground directly behind him. He turned to look but was hit hard by something black driving him against the tree next to him. Mumba had an utter pain growing in his shoulder worse than his foot. Laying on his back, he opened his eyes. His vision greatly impaired by the forced impact against the tree, all he could make out was blurred colors and shapes in the sky. Mumba tried to get up, but the pain begging from his back moving down to his hip drove him back down. He could clearly hear screaming and gun fire, also something else, something that sounded oddly enough like trees cracking then falling to the ground. Chaos ensued around him, he wanted to get up and run but his body was filled with pain.

A horrific roar quieted the screaming and gunfire, the sun was blocked out by a large shadow looming over him. Mumba was only able to identify the blurred object descending upon him as a massive foot the moment before it smashed his head to pieces.

V

The roar reverberated through the forest like a solid blanket of sound. Jane stepped out of her bone tent, revolver in hand, with utmost vigilance. Her eyes darted all over, aggressively scanning the forest. Jane had heard the calls of every animal in the jungle, but this was nothing like she had ever heard before. It was a terrifying sound, creating an unease in her and, obviously, in the forest around her. Even though the terrible wail lasted only a few seconds, its presence still lingered in the air. Jane headed back into her home gathering her things. Placing two revolvers in her belt, strapping her hunting knife to her leg, and arranging supplies into her bag. She fully stocked pouches and pockets of her leather canvas sack with ammo and gun powder, before picking up her elephant rifle. As she stepped back out into the wild, she listened, the void left after the roar was filled once again with that of teeming life. Jane headed in the direction from where she predicted the sound had originated, though it was so loud she was not completely sure. She made her way into the densest part of the forest. Usually, she tried to avoid this area because of ambush and unpredictable terrain, but her instincts pushed her on. There were villagers and shaman that spoke of monstrous sized beasts residing in these parts, things never meant to be seen by the eyes of men. Sniffing the air and following her internal compass the thicket opened slightly revealing a forested hill, looming, and a small stream. Gun pointed forward she adjusted her posture with leg stance wide in a defensive position. Preparing for whatever was to come she moved forward. After a few hours Jane found a large boulder with an overhanging rock edge that could be used for shelter. Deciding this was a good place to camp for the night she set her weapon on the ground and built a fire. She had packed some snakes she caught for the journey and began roasting them on her fire, peeling the charred skin, she picked the cooked meat away from the small bones. With the fire still burning and her stomach full, Jane rested her back against the boulder, picked up her gun and slung it across her chest. She allowed her eyes to rest, partially closed, keeping a high alert to her surroundings. After a couple of hours, she stood looking up at the forest canopy, trying to locate the sun in the sky. It was difficult to judge the time of day this deep in. The ceiling of the forest was a thick blanket of tree trunks, leaves, branches and vines. She was heavily dependent on a strong wind pushing the foliage aside so she could catch a quick glimmer of the sun's rays. Deciding that she possibly had a quarter of full daylight left Jane set out once again trying to make up for lost time. As the day moved on, she could see that the sliver of light that leaked from above began to dwindle. Scanning her location, Jane thought that she would have to find some type of shelter for the night and then head out the next day when the sun was higher in the sky. Ahead there was a thick circle of bushes at the base of a large tree, pushing her way through the brush she lay with her back against the trunk. Tonight, she would not make a fire, the light would only attract the wrong kind of attention. She wrapped herself up in her hide jacket, gun horizontal to her torso, the brim of her hat pulled down over her eyes, Jane let herself doze off into a light sleep. The sun flickered with a stronger force through the forest the following morning. Jane crawled out of the brush noticing the improved visibility. Though the area was still darker than most, she was able to place herself back on the desired course. Continuing on her path she considered what she was doing and where she was going. She had no real understanding of what was driving her but understood there was something she was headed to and she would locate it soon enough. There was a deep hesitation inside of her that told Jane she was not heading toward the source of the sound but toward something else. Something that will shed light on the anxiousness that resonated through the land. After a half day of traveling into the thick forest, down steep hills, and across small rivers she found herself at the top of a ridge leading down to a valley floor. Jane made her way down the embankment, slowly moving backwards, hand over hand on various branches and tree trunks to control her rate of descent. At the bottom of the valley floor she saw that the area was like a trench, clear of brush and trees. The trees on the hills either side of her created a canopy to block out the sky. She could see that clearing was banked right around the steep hill she had just descended and continued around the curve. As Jane made her way around the other side of the hill, she was forced to take a few steps back in shock. A huge hole broke open into the side of the hill at an angle. She stepped into the opening thinking it was at least the height of three men, looking down into the steep decline in the earth, she smelled a stagnant odor permeating from within. The acrid smell stung her nostrils offending her senses, she turned away from the hole to relieve herself of this vile odor when she saw the forest opposite of the hole. The land was flat behind her and there was a long path of trees torn to pieces. Trunks either uprooted right out of the ground or broken in half, splintered fragments sprayed everywhere. Her astonishment returned once again, she couldn't comprehend what was capable of destroying those thick trunks. These were some of the oldest in the land yet they appeared as if something tore through them as if they were small branches. She knew instantly what she was searching for, her inner calling led her to it. The glaring realization hit her that what lay before her was a wound in the heart of Africa. But she had to find out more, she needed to seek council on what this was and what was happening to her land. Turning away from the deep hole in the earth she started back in the direction from which she had come. This time she traveled through the night without stopping, tired and hungry she forced herself on. Another day and a half travel led her to the village of the shaman. The sun was setting on the land with the half orange globe falling behind the far-off mountains. The people in the village seemed occupied as normal but there was a defeated energy in their tasks, something was amiss here as well. As Jane walked through the huts and wooden structures no one paid her any notice, they saw that she was on a mission and did not wish to get in the way. Stepping into the shaman's place of worship was a relief, a small tent like structure that was empty except for a smoldering fire in the center. The shaman sat crossed legged with closed eyes in front of the fire rubbing his hands in the dirt chanting an ancient ritual. Jane placed her gun and backpack off to the side, sitting across the fire from him. She waited for the shaman to complete his prayer, in no rush, it felt good to finally rest her feet and legs.

"You have seen the scar of Africa," spoke the shaman in his native language.

Even though his eyes were still closed Jane nodded.

"The strength of our mother comes from her land and people. The assault on her has weakened her grip," he said.

"What was she holding?" asked Jane.

"There are things from before time, that the first gods sent away to be closed off into mother's bosom."

She sat in silence as he hummed a soft melodic tone.

"Mother's grip has been lost on the monsters of old, due to the outsider's ravage and lust. She is angry and scared for her people. These monsters will punish all," he said softly with a hint of sorrow.

"I need council on what I should do," Jane pleaded.

"See her scar! Feel her pain. Find the broken fragments and piece them together to understand," he said.

The shaman began a long prayer with Jane sitting in front of him wanting him to continue, to shed more light on her questions. The combination of smoke from the fire and travel exhausted her mind. She closed her eyes and let herself lay to her side. Sleep came to her instantly, her thoughts on the roar, the hole and the shaman's words filled her dreams.

'See the Scar.' When she woke the next morning the shaman was gone, her head was clear and she had a better understanding of what she needed to do. Leaving the hut, she found a merchant and traded some food for a torch. She gave a few children in the village some silver then headed off. Before her trek back into the deep, Jane found a river bend and cleaned herself off, ate some charred snake she had left over from the night before and then started out. She dove into the blackness of the jungle, resting for half a day before returning to the opening. Placing her bag and gun near a tree, she grabbed the torch she had just bought. Jane felt uneasy leaving her belongings but knew by the sight of the hole and the area she was in, that this was a place even the most dangerous of animals avoided. She lit the torch, standing at the entrance, the light revealed a portion of the descent but it went so deep that the blackness was overwhelming. Moving slowly over the sloping floor she scanned the dirt cavern, roots hung high above her head, rocks protruded out from the soil walls. Her eyes started to water from the stench that got stronger as she went deeper. Attempting to ignore the smell she couldn't help but think that there was something unnatural about it, preventing her from tuning it out. The angle down was consistent, the dirt floor turning into a muddy mixture as she moved further into the ground. After a long moment she was unsure of how deep she was when suddenly she came upon a rock wall. The size of the cavern got much larger, with her torch revealing what looked like the stone base of a mountain. A large section had been broken open exposing a hollow black abyss. She stepped toward the opening hearing nothing, not even the echo of her breathing. She picked up a small piece of rock that possibly came from the broken aperture and threw it in. No sound, no knock of rock against rock, or splash from hitting water. It was as if the rock was completely taken by the darkness within. With torch in hand she turned away from the endless black void and found large pieces of rock that were thrown all around. Seeing the sections on the floor and then looking back at the opening it was clear something broke out from the darkness. It must have been big and by the thickness of the rock something very strong. She thought of the shaman and looked around, checking over each large chunk of rock she saw that many had paint on them. She grabbed all the pieces she could find with markings (though some were so heavy she had to push them through the wet dirt instead of picking them up) and pieced them together. The completed stone painting before her was that of an elephant, only this elephant was pure black with red eyes. Its trunk elongated into a snake with red eyes and a forked tongue. A cold shiver of horror rose from her feet to her hair, she knew instantly what the image was before her was. This was not some monster arisen, this was something more ancient. She stood for a time in shock staring at the picture, her torch flickered signaling that it was almost spent. Jane headed out before being cast in darkness at the rock edge of this hellish cavity.

VI

Max Gaston Gerlache stood up from behind his desk and walked over to the lifeless fireplace. Placing his hand on the mantle he looked at the handsome lion trophy mounted above it, the king of the jungle silenced in an expression of rage. Gerlache's commander of guards and closest adviser Captain Leon Roger remained standing next to the desk patiently awaiting Gerlache's response to the news he just reported.

Even in the hot temperatures of the Congo, dressed in his full white uniform, Leon Rogers always demanded perfection in his appearance as a member of his military's honor guard.

"When was the last communique from your men in the region?" asked Gerlache wiping off the sweat from his black mustache.

"Six days Jonkheer. Reinforcements were dispensed two nights ago," Roger promptly replied.

"Our English guests must not to be informed of this. It is bad enough we do not have answers to the destruction of our ivory stock. Broken contact with two of our fields can greatly affect the confidence of new investors. This will not please the King."

Gerlache turned and looked at Rogers. He walked back to the desk and lifted a crystal decanter poring himself a drink.

"We need to keep this information to ourselves and remedy our troubles immediately. I want you to take the hired guns and check personally, on the field in the northern front. Our guests will accompany you there, I want you to show them the operations. Following, you will head out and destroy whoever or whatever is massacring my stock in the east," said Gerlache taking a long drink.

"The British business men are to come with us on this hunt?" asked Roger.

"Of course not," scoffed Gerlache, "After you arrive at the fields, one of your men will escort them back here to conclude our business. One of your white men, Leon."

"With all due respect sir, is it completely necessary at the present time to go on with this transaction?" asked Roger.

"With the destruction of the southern field I have a depleting supply of slaves. This is of utmost necessity for the long term. We need to satisfy the King in order to justify our operation. There needs to be an offset of loss."

There was a knock at the door, Gerlache called the person to come in and a slave entered holding his head slightly bowed in order to not make eye contact with Gerlache or Roger. In the slave's deliberate attempt to keep his distance from Captain Roger, it was obvious who he most feared in the room.

"Jonkheer, there are two men waiting downstairs," said the slave.

"You may bring them in," replied Gerlache.

The slave stepped out and a few minutes later two men entered standing side by side in front of the open door.

"Hello Gentlemen, I am Max Gerlache. This is my head of my security forces, Captain Leon Roger, formerly of the Force Publique."

One of the men was a little under six feet tall, he had jet black hair, a thin grey mustache, and a beard. His khaki jacket was buttoned to his neck and tucked into his pants, made from the same material. There was a single pistol attached to his belt and a rifle slung over his shoulder.

"I am Allan Selous, formerly of the British Army," he stated confidently.

The other man was taller, he had short black hair and a thick black beard. He was wearing a khaki vest over a white shirt loose from his pants. Leon Roger noticed, while looking the man over, that he held two pistols on his belt, a knife and a large rifle on his back, the strap across his broad chest. His boots were weathered, having seen some miles, Roger even noticed what might have been dried blood on them.

"Phillip Percival," the man said with a booming voice.

"Let us get on with the business of the day," said Gerlache, "Your reputations' precede you. I have a situation-my elephant herds are being slaughtered. At first both Captain Roger and myself suspected a rival in the ivory trade, but after further investigation we suspect there is an animal attacking and eating them. I believe your expertise can assist in preventing further destruction to my valuable stock," explained Gerlache.

"How many killed Gerlache?" asked Percival.

"Jonkheer!" chided Leon Roger.

Phillip Percival looked at Captain Roger with a sharp gaze. He was not the type of man to be scolded but these were paying customers, he would be prudent and establish a good relationship with this valuable employer.

"My apologies, Jonkheer," Percival corrected.

"No need Mr. Percival. I have had ten destroyed: five females, three bulls and two male calves."

"Any identifiable claw marks or teeth marks to distinguish your predator?" asked Selous.

Gerlache and Roger looked uncomfortably at each other, there was an unspoken uneasiness exchanged between the two that neither Selous or Percival were able to define.

"We have not been able to identify our beast. Accompanied by Captain Roger, you will escort two clients to one of my rubber fields. From there the Captain will bring you to what remains of my herd to observe and decide for yourself."

"I was under the impression that we were here for a hunting engagement, not to play nursemaids to rich businessmen," said Percival with a strong tone of impatience.

"I have hired you for your ability with a gun and for your knowledge of the jungle. Your task is to bring my business partners from my homestead, to one of my fields. From there you will then go on with your pursuit. If there is a grievance say it now so I can find a replacement in the necessary time," responded Gerlache with a tone of impatience.

"No objection Jonkheer," said Selous.

Gerlache looked towards Percival waiting for the American man to raise another objection, but Percival just nodded in consent much to the Belgian's satisfaction.

Leon Roger walked across the room to a book case and pulling out a rolled-up map. Unraveling it, for all to see, across Gerlache's desk, the map was a full layout of Gerlache's land. Various circles positioned all over the map were in red and black ink accompanied by names indicating individual fields across the property. Inside each circle were other markers locating elephant herds, with numbers and other identification keys that were either not important to the hunters or details Leon Roger did not want disclosed.

"You will be traveling along this route to the field located here. From that point Captain Roger will accompany you to the position where the herd was slaughtered."

He pointed on the map tracing the path they would be traveling, then put a metal piece resembling a pawn from a chess set on the spot where the elephants were said to be killed.

Selous looked at the map with intense scrutiny, after a few seconds of familiarizing himself with the different mountain ranges and rivers a familiar point stuck out. He pointed to a spot midpoint between Gerlache's compound and the location marked with the metal marker.

"This is pretty close to an unexplored region of dense forest. Perhaps we should seek Weaver's assistance for that specific area," recommended Selous.

"Haggard has been dead for some time now," Percival explained.

"I do not mean Haggard. It's rumored that his daughter has close ties with a village north of the field where we will be heading. It is a few days added travel but perhaps she could be useful in identifying the beast that is preying on your stock, Jonkheer," Selous recommended.

"That is out of the question," Leon Roger angrily echoed across the room, "We will not seek council from some savage woods woman."

"She is not just some savage, she is the daughter of Haggard Weaver," defended Selous innocently.

"I did not care for, nor will I shed a tear for a barbaric man or his despicable spawn," huffed Leon Roger.

Phillip Percival stepped up to Captain Roger positioning his hand right above one of his pistols. Standing face to face the height and mass difference between the two men was staggering. Leon Roger, though at a size disadvantage, steadied his hand close to his knife handle waiting for Percival to make the first move.

"I give respect to Jonkheer Gerlache as I am a guest in his home. Make no mistake that the courtesy is afforded to you as well Leon. However, Haggard Weaver earned his reverence on this continent. If I hear another word of contempt for him out of your mouth, we will have words between us," Percival said with a heated yet steady bellow that silenced the room.

Both men peered into the other's eyes. Leon Roger, holding back from any sign of intimidation, refusing to be backed down, especially by the likes of Phillip Percival. Captain Roger had his own story as a man of cruelty, but Phillip Percival had notoriety as a 'great white hunter'. In the seconds that passed Leon Roger considered his options but was not ready to test Percival's quick American temper, especially without a pistol on hand.

"My good men let us cool our tongues with a drink and fill our bellies with a hearty meal," interrupted Gerlache, "I have hired you on the basis of your bravery and professionalism. I can see that both hold true and my time and money is well spent."

Percival held the gaze of Leon Roger a few seconds longer, then turned and looked at Gerlache ignoring the continuous scowl from the Captain.

"You three shall leave tomorrow with our anticipated guests. I would be honored if you would walk around and enjoy my grounds until then. My servants are at your beckoning and can arrange anything you desire," Gerlache said with a gregarious wave of the hand.

"Thank you Jonkheer Gerlache," said Selous.

"Much appreciated sir," added Percival.

There was another knock at the open door, a different slave entered the room with his head bowed.

"Jonkheer, there is a caravan of eight men approaching the western gate," said the man in a defeatist tone.

"That must be the English fellows from South America," Gerlache said with a forced smile.

"Please gentleman I implore you to enjoy the rest of your day. I have other matters I must attend to. We will reconvene at dinner."

Percival and Selous nodded in agreement before leaving the room, they were intercepted outside of the office by two slaves who directed them to their opposing rooms.

When Gerlache and Leon Roger were alone once again, Gerlache gave his head of security a strong disagreeable look.

"Captain, let us agree not to antagonize the hired men with rifles?"

Before Leon Roger could respond Gerlache turned to face the window behind his desk then lifted his hand in a dismissive manner signaling for the Captain to leave. With a hidden surge of anger Leon Roger did an about face leaving the office. Outside of the door he attempted to quell the surging rage building inside of him. First the American dares to challenge him, then Jonkheer takes the outsider's position. Leon Roger felt this was an afront to the dignity of a man in his position. If he were still in the military such disrespect would not go unchallenged. At that moment Captain Roger had to remind himself that he was no longer in the service of the Belgian Military. It was true that he still had contacts and close connections, but he had chosen the private sector. This was the price he paid for the large sums of money he was receiving from King Leopold and Jonkheer Gerlache; every so often his gravitas would have to take one on the chin. Leon Roger held his breath and counted backward waiting for the red heat in his head to subside. When the storm dissipated, he continued down the hall to resume the business of the day.

- - - -

As the group approached the compound, John couldn't help but feel amazed by the sheer size of the area. For most of the day they traveled over a beaten path carved out of the jungle floor, exiting the forest they came upon a vast open expanse. A partial wooden fence encompassed a shoddy village built for slaves who worked the grounds of Gerlache's property. John thought it was the home of a large tribe but as they drew closer, he noticed the poor structure design and unkept conditions. The caravan moved further onto the grounds and then the huge estate house, built on the top of an overlooking hill, became visible. It was an architectural marvel that such a building could be constructed in what felt like one of the most secluded regions of the world, deep in the center of Africa. Gerlache's mansion was a two-storied white building with a small attic that had a dormer window under a crimson roof. The first floor was encompassed by a porch that was decorated with arching pillars throughout. Tables and chairs were neatly placed giving off a welcoming aura. The second floor had a porch on two sides with large French doors overlooking the vast land.

John reminded himself he was not there to marvel over Gerlache's luxurious lifestyle, his duty was to observe and document the slaves that made this operation functional.

Making mental notes of the living conditions around him, John began to take account of how many individuals he saw, as well as their lifestyle and physical appearance. As they moved he burned these observations into his memory in order to log them into his diary later when he was alone.

Men, women and children alike through the village hustled about in unfit clothing that clung awkwardly to their bodies as they hurried past the large group. They worked in the blistering sun, their backs bent as many carried heavy buckets of water or

pushed carriages filled with baskets of food, all appeared to operate around the main house.

"These conditions are horrendous," John whispered to
Michael.

"Yes, but they are not consistent with what was described in
our briefings," Michael replied.

"These conditions are better than those in the field, but
make no mistake, these people live in constant terror. We are only
seeing those who act accordingly, the ones who misbehave are
sent to do the grueling work on the land or possibly they are never
seen again," whispered Monroe overhearing the comments.

As he spoke, Monroe made a point not to be seen talking
directly to Michael and John by any of the slaves around them. If
they suspected Monroe of speaking to the men as equals it might
be reported to their holders who would of course alert Captain
Roger or his subordinates. This would potentially have the consequence of exposing their whole operation, and possibly forfeiting
their lives.

John wanted to speak to one of the slaves who passed but
Monroe objected intensely, he explained that even attempting
to communicate with one of the slaves would raise suspicion.
Constant fear and unease are tools used to destroy any form of
unity. He cautiously explained that the ground masters encouraged them to inform on one another for favors or rewards.

The route they followed bisected a much larger road packed with dead grass, this appeared to be the major vein of travel that crisscrossed with all the other routes throughout the compound.

"This is where our communication must stop completely. I will begin my part as your servant," said Monroe bowing his head.

They looked at him wanting to display some sort of appreciation. Over the course of their travel, since the moment they met in Lagos, they had developed a strong relationship with Monroe. But, for their own good, heeded his instructions.

"From here you both walk ahead at a distance. We will carry the rest of the supplies ourselves. When we get close to the main house, the six of us will be stopped by staff and prohibited from entering the surrounding area. From there we will be brought to a place designated for the slaves who work inside the mansion."

John looked at Monroe with distress, hoping to object to the idea of Monroe and the other men being far from hand.

"Will that not put you in danger?" asked John.

"Do not worry about us. The both of you may very well be in greater of danger," Monroe said still looking toward the ground blocking view of his mouth.

"That is not especially comforting," Michael said with a hint of worry.

"Keep your attention directed at the task. Before you know it, you will be sipping tea on a Royal Mail Service back home," Monroe tried to assure them.

"Even less encouraging Monroe," proclaimed Michael.

Monroe could see the tension rising in Michael and John, he thought of a suitable anecdote that might help the men with their troubles.

"There are many times as a proxy for Parliament that I find myself at odds and looking for courage. Whenever tribulations arise, I would bring my thoughts back to rainy days in England. I remember studying as a boy, looking out of the window while I sat at my desk. Though it was an unwelcoming, adopted land, it was still home," he spoke softly his eyes watery.

- - - -

Michael and John were escorted into the house by one of Gerlache's slaves, they were brought into what they assumed was the Trophy Room.

A large suite with French doors that opened to two elegant sofas positioned opposite each other with a small table in between. An elephant head, with crossing ivory tusks under it, facing the entrance, stared at them from the far wall. A stuffed male lion was positioned on its hind legs to the left of the elephant head and a ferociously positioned tiger on its hind legs to the right.

Decorating the entire room were other types of trophies such as zebras, gazelles, and a water buffalo along with random fowls positioned near the ceiling.

John and Michael sat on the same couch in silence, looking around at the various trophy animals. It was eerily uncomfortable, feeling like a strange homage to death and dominance over Africa's native wildlife.

A short time later the doors swung open and Gerlache entered, he looked older and more tired compared to the photo they had been shown. A portly man, Gerlache wasn't wearing a hat and his graying hair was combed back. He still had his black mustache and wore a dark navy suit with a gold sash across his chest.

"I am sorry to have kept you waiting gentleman. I am Jonkheer Gaston Gerlache. You must be spent after your long trip, may I offer you a drink?" he boomed in a genuine tone.

Neither Michael nor John was in the mood for a drink due to their nervousness, but both felt they should accept the offer to keep up the part they were playing.

Gerlache ordered the slave standing at the door to bring in a tray of the house's finest spirits.

"Jonkheer Gerlache, I would like to thank you for your most gracious hospitality. I am Michael Allen, proprietor of the Peruvian National Company. This is John Alpert, my Chief of Operations," Michael said standing up from the couch.

"Just a fancy word for bookkeeper," John said forcing himself to create a wide smile, standing from the coach after Michael.

Gerlache laughed at the comment sitting down on the opposite couch appearing more at ease. Once he was seated, Michael and John followed sitting back down.

"I hope your journey was not trying. I would have liked to meet you closer to the boat but I am afraid my welcome in Lagos is uncertain," said Gerlache.

"Our journey was pleasant and uneventful, Jonkheer. We arranged for a group of servants to assist us on the trip. Unfortunately, Lagos is a free area so we had to pay a higher price than we are accustomed to. That is why I bring John of course, to make sure the cost is manageable," Michael spoke creating the same fake smile as John had previously.

Though unknown to Gerlache, Michael and John began to feel a little more at ease. They fell into their desired parts beautifully and for a moment did not feel as if they were sitting across from a very powerful and very dangerous man.

The slave returned holding a silver tray with glass cups and two bottles. He placed the tray neatly on the table then lifted one of the bottles presenting the label to each of the three men. Gerlache looked at John and Michael, raising an open palm to verify their acceptance, they both nodded in approval at the quality of the brand. The slave opened the bottle preparing three drinks then stood near Gerlache until he was waived away in a silent dismissal. When the doors were closed, they continued their discussion.

"If it pleases you, we can keep this brief. I am sure that you are eager to be shown to your quarters to rest a bit. We shall reconvene tonight and go into further detail over dinner this evening," said Gerlache.

"That sounds agreeable. We appreciate your understanding of our fatigue," replied Michael.

"Mr. Allen, I understand you are vested in rubber trade out west. With the information you shared through telegraph it is obvious you operate a profitable enterprise on the smaller end, of course. Would it be proper to assume this is to keep your transactions away from government oversite?" asked Gerlache.

"Please, call me Michael. That is correct Jonkheer, I am a private businessman. I have kept my capital dealings very scant on the British mainland. I hold small investments specifically in boutique businesses, to protect from catching unwanted attention from Her Majesty's government as well as from the Americans," elaborated Michael.

"That is quite understandable," Gerlache said lifting his glass for a sip.

"I have a growing workforce of slaves with only so much land to cultivate. I can always expand, but that may bring undesired inquiry. My company's position is to keep extraction at its current size but to grow by utilizing resources on hand," Michael continued

While both men were talking, John was studying Gerlache hoping not to make it conspicuous. He was attempting to decipher when the Belgian was either lying or withholding information.

"We may be able to help one another, Michael. Restrictions placed on the slave trade in this region have caused limitations on the availability of labor. You on the other hand appear to have more labor but less cultivable land," said Gerlache.

"That is correct Jonkheer," Michael agreed.

"Perhaps we could strike an agreement on shipment of labor from the west."

"That would be acceptable. How many slaves do you currently have in the field at this time?" asked Michael.

"I have 4,000 slaves working in my fields not including those in the ivory herds or on my land here," replied Gerlache.

John made the assumption that he was lying, feeling that he was greatly inflating the numbers. What made John curious was the reason behind the lie, since Gerlache was positioning to buy more slaves.

"How much yield of rubber do your fields produce?" asked Michael.

John was beginning to admire the art Michael was displaying. He was confident and knowledgeable, able to ask questions that Gerlache was anticipating.

"Combined, my fields produce over 11 tons a year of mid to high grade quality," boasted Gerlache with a rise of his chin.

"How many slaves do you need to keep above abatement to continue productivity?" asked Michael.

"I lose 200 a year due to various factors, that figure excludes offspring incorporated yearly once they reach working age. Now, I do require a strong and reliable workforce, I have heard though that the South American slaves are not as obedient and are more aggressive than the Africans," stated Gerlache.

"Aggression is a trait that can be bred and tamed for use in the field. The problem you will face is not the ability to control them but cooperation among your slaves born here. Conflict could become an issue," said Michael.

"I do not foresee that as an issue. I have members of the Force Publique as my arms in the field," Gerlache stated proudly.

John became distracted with the subject of the conversation. They were talking about people of course but here they were discussing them as if they were livestock.

"John, do you have any input considering logistics?" Michael said crossing his legs with drink in hand.

John quickly snapped himself out of the uncomfortable daze and attempted to push back the offensive feeling building in his gut and to continue with the task.

"We need to see figures on transportation costs. It is also necessary to consider cost for paying off ports at departure and entry points. Numbers would have to be calculated for depreciation during shipment."

John was astonished with himself. He attempted to hold his disgust for the part he was playing and hold on to the truth that the words he spoke did not represent his feelings.

"All the intricate numbers can be discussed later. We will factor in those costs when negotiating price per unit. What would you require on your end?" asked Gerlache.

"Other than financial gain I am interested in your quality of rubber trees. I was told of their exquisite standards which could be beneficial to increasing my profits out west. If I can extract a higher grade of substance, I could justifiably increase prices to my buyers," said Michael.

"I have the highest quality rubber. You will not be disappointed," smiled Gerlache "Tomorrow a couple of my men will be heading out to one of my fields. Unfortunately, I am unable to attend but I could arrange for you to accompany them and get a firsthand look. While you are there take a look at my labor force so you have a better understanding of my purchase requirements."

John looked at Michael nervously and it appeared to Gerlache that there was hesitation between them both.

"You will be escorted by my Security Chief Captain Leon Roger and two of Africa's finest sportsman," Gerlache continued, attempting to ease their apprehension.

"You will not be going with us?" inquired John.

He spoke out of reaction and immediately considered his statement out of place. He forgot that Michael was the man in charge, acting too eagerly trying to reveal the situation Gerlache was manipulating.

"I have to attend to many guests and meetings, dignitaries from foreign lands that are due to arrive within a few days. It is only a two-day journey, when you return this arrangement will have my fullest attention," Gerlache assured.

"I would prefer to see the rubber quality before I agree to substitute my crops," Micheal said attempting to amend the error John almost created.

"Then we are on terms I assume?" Gerlache asked raising both hands with palms facing up.

"We are, Jonkheer. Will you see that our servants are cared for during our absence? I would rather avoid any unpleasant inquiry once I return to Lagos," explained Michael.

"Yes, their wellbeing is guaranteed, I assure you. Shall we continue this discussion at dinner when you are well rested?" he said standing up.

The slaves outside of the room must has received prior instructions to enter once Gerlache stood since the doors opened immediately revealing two men standing by.

"That would be agreeable Jonkheer Gerlache," said Michael.

"My servants will show you to your individual rooms and will assist you in anything you require."

Both men followed the slaves up the grand staircase and down long elegantly decorated hallways to their rooms. After entering his quarters John sat on the bed fighting off the increasing weight of physical exhaustion. He looked at the dresser against one of the walls and remembered the letter. A sudden urgency washed over him, a desire to continue writing to his sister. It was left unfinished in his bag, the thought of physically getting up to retrieve it then to sit down to write pushed him even further to the edge of sleep. He thought that maybe a trip across the hall to Michael might wake him up.

When John knocked on the door Michael called to him from inside to enter. John walked in finding Michael lying on the large bed, enjoying the luxurious comfort.

"That was extremely odd at how easy it was to gain access to his fields," whispered John easing the door shut behind him.

"I do find it strange how quickly he dismissed us. I assumed it would take a day or two of negotiations to see his operation," said Michael.

"I think something is amiss here. I feel he greatly exaggerated his numbers of men in the field, now he wants us to go out and see them," John said with a worried tone.

"I agree, that may be why he is eager for us to depart. Could be due to some fallacy that could potentially collapse our agreement," Michael said with a pensive look.

"Any thoughts to what that might be?" asked John.

"Patience may be our only avenue. If he is fearful of losing this exchange then he is not suspicious of us. We have the upper hand and will be easier for us to collect proof," Michel explained.

"If there were only a way to get a message to Monroe, let him know to keep an eye out for anything questionable while we are away," John said, distraught.

They both sat and stared uneasily out of the open window at the sun setting over the distant green mountains. It was the most extraordinary sight mired by the crushing stress caused by the unfolding events. John returned to his room to unpack and put on clean cloths, preparing for dinner. In the back of his mind he dreaded the unavoidable first encounter with Captain Leon Roger.

VII

In the main dining room, there was a long table set with a white cloth. Candles and vases were positioned in alternating places down its center.

John and Michael sat on one side with their soon to be escorts sitting directly across from them. John could not help but see the contrasting yet similar aspects between the two men. One was polished and refined, though his history was clearly written in his eyes. The man had his hands placed on the table, John could see them clearly, they were weathered with heavy experience. The other man's appearance did not conceal his probably colorful background. His facial expression was standoffish, thoroughly indicating that clearly it was improper to ask. John could see these were seasoned men, it was in their mannerisms and posture. Nothing was more transparent than their eyes. Their eyes told stories of years spent in the darkest areas of the world, holding tales that would probably turn John's hair white. He considered, with a bit of arrogance, if either had ever before sat at an elegant table like this. When this thought was marinating, John admitted to himself that he had never before sat at an excessively luxurious table like this either.

Drinks were served as the four men awaited their host. Table conversation never started and the growing silence was becoming increasingly awkward. True to his outgoing nature it was Michael who attempted to crack the ice in the cold room.

"I suppose you men will be our escorts in the field tomorrow?" he asked curiously.

This comment appeared to not sit well with either of them, they looked at each other with expressions of unhappy surrender.

"That is correct. We will be traveling with you into the jungle tomorrow," responded the more tacked of the two. "I am Alan Selous."

"Pleased to make your acquaintance. I am Michael Allen and this is my business associate John Alpert. You are British born, Mr. Selous?" Michael inquired.

The way Michael posed the question made John a little uncomfortable, these men did not appear about whom you could make suppositions.

"Yes, I served as an Army Officer for many years. We were stationed in the southern region. I have not lived on English soil for a while, but I do keep a family in Salisbury," he replied.

"Interesting, and how about you sir?" Michael said directly acknowledging Percival.

"Phillip Percival. That is about as much as I care to share right now," he answered with a monotone.

"An American, that is very well. It is a pleasure to make both your acquaintances considering the brevity of time we will be spending before our journey," Michael said with his customary smile.

John could tell this was Michael's way of relieving the tension building at the table, but wished he would not push these men any further.

"What business do you gentleman have in the heart of darkness?" Selous inquired.

Much to John's relief is seemed that Michael's attempt worked in luring at least one of these men into polite conversation, the tension did seem a bit more relaxed.

"I own a Peruvian Rubber company. I am attempting to expand my business by negotiating a potential deal with Jonkheer Gerlache," Michael explained.

At that moment two men entered the hall, John immediately recognized Gerlache. When he saw the other man, his heart felt heavy and dropped in his gut. He instantly recognized Captain Leon Roger, from the picture back in England. The iciness of the photograph reflected the cold presence of the man. John attempted to control the coursing shiver surging through his body.

Gerlache sat at the end of the table facing all his guests and Leon Roger sat next to him, adjacent to Allan Selous and Phillip Percival.

The night went mostly without incident. Most of the conversations were exchanged, predominantly, among Gerlache, John and Michael.

Pleasantries were spoken and John found Allan Selous quite charming but couldn't decide if it was due to Selous' personality or simply because he was the only other Englishman in the room besides himself and Michael.

Percival, a man of few words, did not speak much. John did not feel that it was discourteous, he was simply direct and clear to the point. When they began dabbling in a discussion of African politics, Percival always answered with a very strong point of view but without causing controversy. Though John thought that could be because Phillip Percival was the type of man with whom others would purposely avoid controversy.

John, at first encounter, wasn't sure how it would to be on a two-day travel with these men, but gradually felt it would not be too difficult and warmed up to the idea. He believed deeply that they would be safer with Percival and Selous guiding them through unfamiliar territory. He secretly hoped Percival would open up once they were in the jungle, and could only imagine what insights he held. John looked forward to hearing a recanting of stories from his journeys across Africa. It was certainly clear

Phillip Percival was out of his element sitting at a table with silver candle holders and gold rimmed plates. John assumed the man was more comfortable roughing it in the jungle with nothing but a fire and his rifle on hand.

Captain Roger held a strong silence that created a menacing feel to John. In his chair he watched every man who spoke with a hawkish gaze, looking as if he were attempting to identify a single weakness or deception every time someone spoke. It wasn't until they were almost finished with desert that he decided to speak up and as John feared, his inquiry was directed toward John and Michael.

"Mr. Allen, you and Mr. Alpert have been business partners a long time?" inserted Roger.

"We actually were acquainted when studying at Oxford. I worked in a telegraph company after I finished university and John was bookkeeping for an antiquities trader," Michael explained with a half-truth.

"How did you become connected financially?" pressed Roger.

"It wasn't until my sister passed away, Michael was engaged to marry her. After her unexpected death, Michael telegraphed me to say he was finished with England. He requested my companionship across the Atlantic to possibly escape the painful memories," added John.

"I am sorry for your loss sir," Gerlache said, it seemed completely sincere.

"That is kind of you Jonkheer but it was a long time ago. I have been able to overcome my grief with success. The women in South America have also been quite helpful as… shall I say mental therapy," Michael said with a quirky smile, lifting his glass to the men.

He attempted to avoid eye contact with John following his previous remark hoping it did not press him in any way. Gerlache emitted a loud chuckle and Selous smiled in what was probably a polite reaction, Percival and Captain Roger made no attempt in acknowledging his witty insinuation.

"Pardon me for asking Mr. Allen but was your fiance's death the precursor for your broken loyalty to England?" Leon Roger continued with an unemotional look.

"I have no real broken loyalty to England. However, the current political environment, in England as well as in America, frown on how I am living," Michael coolly elaborated.

"I have never had to make that decision since the King and I are mutual financial benefactors. I must comment I do admire your long-term choice Michael," Gerlache replied.

"You pay no tariffs to your home country?" Leon Roger continued with the steely questions.

"Well I must admit I am not the numbers man. As Chief Operator John takes care of the accounting. I just sign the checks and get angry when business is not as profitable as my lifestyle requires," smiled Michael.

"Not to disclose too many company secrets but various accounts are placed along multiple shores. It allows me to move the company's money without raising suspicion from greedy governments. Our major field is near the center of South America therefor our primary holding is in Peru. It is more favorable to businesses like ours," John elaborated, relieving Michael of further inquiry.

"If the Jonkheer was to further commerce with Peruvian National how do you plan on hiding the transaction?" Leon Roger asked.

It appeared this question most pleased Gerlache, he nodded his head towards the Captain then turned his attention to John awaiting a solid reply. It became clear who the real intelligence was, Gerlache was obviously the man in charge but Captain Roger was the one who ensured the survival of their operation.

"Again, I rather not divulge too many of the company secrets," insisted John.

This answer seemed to displease Gerlache who looked towards Captain Roger to see how he would react to this refusal. Michael picked up on tension building and was able to defuse the situation quickly.

"Come now John, we are all friends here. I highly doubt the Jonkheer or Captain Roger are in the least interested in selling our company secrets. I cannot imagine who would be interested in the boring economics anyway," Michael said with a quick laugh looking at Gerlache.

The Jonkheer smiled in a silent agreement that clearly stated he was bored by the details of fiscal policy, but Leon Roger showed no tilt in his query and continued to stare at John with a face that demanded answers.

"To begin with I divest properties under surnames and sell them off to banks in England that have no interest in the origins of purchase. Their sole concern is that there are no legalities blocking the transaction. To elaborate, before we made the venture out here, I discovered a South American bank being built in Lagos. After Michael and the Jonkheer conclude their agreement I would arrange for the money to be transfered into the Lagos bank to keep the transaction private," John said directing his answer to Gerlache.

Though he was looking to the Jonkheer, he knew the real person he needed to sell his response to was Leon Roger. John was surprised by his quick reaction, the information he had absorbed during his short time in Lagos helped immensely in deflecting Leon Roger's unofficial interrogation.

"That is quite enough financial talk at the table. Captain, this type of probing is clearly inappropriate at the current time. I have done my due diligence into their background and that is satisfactory enough. In addition, all this talk must be boring to Mr. Selous and Mr. Percival," Gerlache echoed across the room.

"I find it quite interesting," said Selous.

"I have no valuable opinion," Percival replied with an uncaring tone.

"Jonkheer, Mr. Selous was elaborating on his service in the British Army prior to you and Captain Roger arriving," Michael said hoping to change the subject.

"Indeed, you were an Officer. That is correct?" Gerlache said turning his head to the two hunters.

"That is indeed correct sir. I met a woman and decided to leave the service. Now I hunt game and fortunes promised throughout the land," Selous said looking around giving his attention to each person equally.

"What type of game to you favor Mr. Selous?" asked John.

"Whatever the market requires, furs of cheetah and pelts of lions. I do find the occasional request to destroy a problematic rogue."

"I apologize, did you say rouge?" Michael asked looking curiously at Selous.

"It is a term used to describe a menacing animal responsible for human casualties. For instance, last summer I was commissioned to dispense two lionesses responsible for many deaths on a railway construction in Tsavo," Selous explained.

"Similar to the situation you are facing now Jonkheer?" Percival asked with an aggressive tone.

Since the man remained silent for most of the discussion this question was a surprise to everyone especially Gerlache, who did not look eager to answer.

"Yes, well that is why I have you men here to assist me," Gerlache said quickly, hoping not to elaborate further.

"I apologize Jonkheer if our arrival coincided with difficulties you are currently handling."

John spoke hoping this would open the door for further discussion into what Percival was alluding to.

"Your arrival is most welcome, John. I have had an issue with a beast of my own attacking the ivory stock. Nothing with great financial harm, but causing enough of an annoyance."

Following his reply, Gerlache gave Percival a stern look of disapproval.

Michael was clearly interested in the conversation, pressing on with another question, "Lions would openly attack an elephant of size?"

"Circumstances could push any animal to act out, for instance, starvation, desperation, even fits of rage. In my years I have learned Africa can hold endless amounts of mystery. One is never at a loss for surprise," Percival explained, "Have you men ever experience the depths of Africa?"

It was clear Percival was attempting to alter the course of the conversation in order to appease Gerlache.

"I found our journey from Lagos most trying. The closest either John or myself have experienced for comparison are survey expeditions in South America. These previous travels forced us to be without comforts we are accustomed to," Michael replied.

"I do not mean traveling with servants across the beaten path. We are going deep into the thicket and coming close to the edge of uncharted regions. We will be touching danger right on the back," Percival spoke with eyes burning directly at Michael.

The hunter picked up his glass and took a large sip of wine, placing his drink in its original spot he then lifted his napkin to wipe the droplets left on his mustache.

"Jonkheer, perhaps it is prudent that Selous and I take some time to go over the fine lines of survival skills with these men. This would greatly alleviate the pressure on us, it would also build up their confidence as we make our way in the field," Percival recommended.

"A splendid idea Phillip, why not get more comfortable in the lounge with cigars and stiff drinks," Gerlache said with a broad smile.

Selous looked to be in agreement with this idea, John and Michael nodded their heads in a silent consent. The only person who made no facial gesture was Leon Roger, with his cold gaze, his wariness was louder than any words could express. Even though Gerlache was jovial and in good manner it was the unreadable Captain Roger who drove doubt through John's hopeful spirit.

VIII

The day they left for the plantation was a trying one, with a scorching sun beating down on their heads. John couldn't shake the deep feeling in his bones that they were unprepared. The questions from Leon Roger the night before, thick mistrust growing under the surface, rattled his confidence in their current task. On their journey to Jonkeer's mansion they had Monroe with them, which John began to feel may have created an artificial sense of security. At present they were parading out in the elements under a mask of false pretense, with two men whose allegiance they were ignorant of, and one whom they absolutely didn't trust.

Hours passed traveling through grassy hills, a patch of dirty tundra and into a thicket of dense forest, where John noticed that the chaotic arrangement of trees became a lot more uniform. Pulling himself out of a foggy mindset of fatigue, he could see that the congruently lined trees were Sharingas or also known as rubber plants.

He attempted to educate himself with research in preparing for this venture, when faced with the flora he observed only in books he thought they were not as tall as he had expected. John desperately hoped his knowledge on the product would not be put to the test and anticipated Michael was a little more versed on the subject.

"These look to be younglings. How many more seasons before they are cultivated?" inquired Michael.

Letting out an internal sigh of relief, John was once again amazed at Michael for his insightful question that covertly sold his faux expertise.

Captain Roger at first ignored the inquiry as he led the group, Michael looked at Leon Roger thinking the man may not have heard him. After a short time, John then looked in his direction trying to decipher if Captain Roger was purposely ignoring Michael. After a moment of awkward silence, he answered the question left out in the air.

"They could be milked now but the quality of product would be lacking. Another two or three more seasons would show a ripe product," replied Leon Roger.

"I like their flowering. The leaves look healthy. How are the seeds?" Michael pressed with a follow up.

Before Captain Roger could either create another unnecessary pause, or reply with his customary snarky tone a strong wind picked up carrying with it the unmistakable smell of decay.

The putrid odor of death was obvious to all the men. Percival and Selous immediately removed their rifles which were slung over their shoulders, looking all around, they scanned the area. Michael and John stopped only a few yards behind them attempting to follow their tracking eyes looking for what the hunters might be searching for.

It was Leon Roger who, in the motion of a deadly predator, did not move. He stood like a marble statue staring straight ahead, never going for his gun, never breaking his line of sight. Percival was the first to take notice and looked forward in the direction that Leon Roger was locked on.

"What in the lord's name?" he proclaimed.

Michael and John followed their line of sight but couldn't find anything irregular in what they saw. The group continued forward with all five men looking in the exact same direction. The stench of decomposition grew more potent and, at the moment it became unbearable, was when both John and Michael saw what the other men had observed a few yards earlier.

The trees ahead were obviously much larger and older than the ones they had passed through, though these looked like a giant storm dropped dead center on top of them.

A large section of the forest had been torn apart, trunks ripped from their base, large chunks ripped open like bloody wounds oozing hardening white liquid rubber.

Attempting to comprehend what could have destroyed such a large area of the forest, John's attention was attracted to the loud buzzing of hundreds, if not thousands, of flies. His eyes darted all over to locate their origin, the flies drew his sight to the bodies.

There were hundreds of them strewn all over the broken area. Limbs protruded from the ground laying near smashed torsos, reduced to nothing more than hunks of broken flesh. Bodies hung from the branches of partially fallen trees. Blood was everywhere, shattered bones mixed with the remnants of broken wood. The sheer carnage in the area made it difficult to count how many bodies there were but John knew whatever had occurred left no survivors.

This was a massacre, was the only thought that came across John's mind.

"Captain Roger!" Selous called to him with a fallen tree laying between them.

"Was it Jumma Tibbu?" asked Percival.

"He wouldn't have slaughtered the slaves like this. This would not have been a beneficial attack for the Zanzibari Sultan," replied Selous.

"This is more of a statement. Perhaps Mahdist rebels or that scoundrel Count Hippolyte," sneered Leon Roger through the baring teeth of growing fury.

"Is the Count not part of the Anti-Slavery Society? How would slaughtering all these men help their cause?" asked Michael.

"These were not MEN. They were slaves, property of the kingdom," Captain Roger angrily barked towards Michael with a look of ever-increasing rage.

Michael realized he almost exposed their deception, at that point he decided to play the part of partisan politics in an attempt to ease the growing tension.

"My apologies, Captain. I was only considering what could have rationally happened to the Jonkeer's assets," Michael humbly said with a slight bow of the head.

Leon Roger gave Michael and John a questioning look but his attention was quickly drawn back to the anarchy of the surrounding area. Selous and Percival held their rifles in a defensive manner, stepping over the vast disbursement of bodies and large chunks of fallen trees. Both men were looking for tracks or any clues that could shed light on revealing the cause of this slaughter.

John moved around looking at the horrendous sights displayed all around him. Corpses broken across tree trunks, heads crushed into the ground, and in more than one instance bodies appeared torn apart. He was shocked trying to mentally grasp who, or what could have done this. Living in a large city far away from here, he realized how blinded he was to the atrocities that the world hid in its darkest regions. He read about the horrors in countries far from his home, but standing in this field, for the first time in his life he was privy to witness the evils that exist. John looked across the field, seeing for the first time the darkness of the forest behind the trees. As he imagined what kind of monsters moved amongst the shadows, he thought he could actually see the darkness materialize into one of these creatures. He brought his hand to his eyes, wiping the sweat dripping from his forehead to clear his vision. When he looked back the thing he saw was still there. Not so far off, at the edge of the forest, he imagined he could see the head of a large bull elephant. The monster's skin black and scaly almost reptilian, two large tusks protruding from its face lined with veiny cracks, each almost a meter and a half in length.

John could clearly make out in the depths of its deep black eyes a red shining pinpoint dot.

The creature let out a deafening roar revealing that this was no manifestation of John's imagination, the rest of the group turned to see just as the beast began to charge at John.

Frozen in fear he could not move, he was locked in the sight of those cavernous eyes.

Right at the moment he convinced himself that this was when he was going to die, trampled by the horrendous beast, a blast shook the forest. A bullet tore through the creatures left ear tearing away a small chunk. The monster roared in retaliation then altered its trajectory to the right crashing across the field and into the forest with an unnatural speed. In its wake, tearing apart trees and branches, leaving behind a scar of destruction at the jungle edge.

Still in disbelief at what had just occurred, John looked to where the shot was fired. There was a woman, wearing a large brimmed hat, holding an enormous rifle pressed to her shoulder, she was still aiming in the direction of the creature, expecting it to return.

John looked her over seeing that she donned a weathered khaki jacket, a white cloth shirt underneath, and khaki pants that were tucked into boots caked with mud.

John fell to his knees and emptied the contents of his stomach. The sheer intensity of the situation was too much for his nerves, creating a dizzy spell. Sitting up in a kneeling position, he placed his hands on his thighs, attempting to stand up. Someone stepped in front him blocking the rays from the beating sun.

John looked up at the silhouette of the women who held out her hand as a gesture to assist him to his feet. He reached out feeling how rough and callused her palms were. When she squeezed, pulling him up, he was amazed at her strength.

Percival, Selous and Michael hurried over to both John and the women as Leon Roger kept a far distance behind.

She slung her rifle by its strap over her shoulder and directed her attention to the men approaching.

"It will circle back. We need to move out of this area now," she said with a tone of confidence.

"Why did it charge like that?" asked Michael panting from the run over.

"I have never seen a bull like that before," Percival explained looking directly at the women.

"Do you think it was capable of causing this?" Selous asked looking at the ruination all around.

"It caused this. From the tracks I observed around the area it has been stalking within range for the last day," she stated.

"A bull would not do this, it's unnatural," replied Selous with astonishment.

"It's not a bull," the women said flatly.

"What was it then?" John interjected, wiping his mouth clean of residue.

"I feel it has been waiting for your group to arrive. When you were near the center, clear of the forest edge was when it attacked."

"You are trespassing on private land. I demand you vacate immediately or I will have to shoot you in the name of King Leopold the Second," cried Captain Roger from behind the men.

He stood at a distance with a defensive stance, the others turned in his direction unsure if his proclamation was serious. The women raised her head with a menacing glare in his direction, she hovered her hand over the handle of the pistol in her belt and waited for Leon Roger's next move.

Percival stepped between the two, raising his arms in a blocking gesture.

"No need for aggression here. She just saved or tails," Percival boomed at Leon Roger.

He turned towards the women, she tilted her head up revealing a strong face, her dark brown eyes locked with those of Percival. John could see she had long hair but it was tucked away under her hat.

"Jane Weaver?" Percival asked.

"That I am," she said.

"I am Phillip Percival. It is an honor to meet the kin of Haggard Weaver."

He held out his hand to receive a shake, Jane looked at him skeptically and took his invitation with a firm grasp.

"His demise is a deep loss for this land. I give you my condolences," he said with a gruff empathy.

"It was a long time ago. Your solace is unnecessary but appreciated," Jane replied.

"I agree with Miss Weaver, we should move post haste. An unwarranted attack like that will most likely result in another. It, without question, wants us to leave this area," said Selous with a deep concern.

"It was a Grootslang," Jane said coldly.

Percival and Selous looked at her with astonishment, they could not believe what she just proclaimed. Michael and John exchanged glances then focused on the other three quizzically, hoping they would shed light on what she meant and why the hunters now wore a look of fear.

"Savage superstition," yelled Leon Roger, "I will not stand here any longer and expose myself to the raving tales of a barbarian."

Jane appeared to be unfazed by the obvious insult, she turned and moved towards the area of the jungle from which she had come. John saw that it was the opposite direction of where the monster had retreated.

"Captain Roger, we should get these men back to the compound for their protection. Ravenous bull or not, it will return," Percival stated, turning towards the fuming Leon Roger.

"We need to check on the other fields. There are two more locations to the west that should be secured before we head back," demanded the Captain.

"Those are gone as well," Jane noted, standing by the edge of the forest.

"No one asked you vile girl," Captain Roger boomed in reply.

"I do not believe the Jonkeer would want his business partners being put at risk with a trek out west, Sir," Percival voiced with a patronizing tone.

"Without securing his other assets there is no partnership. Now I believe that you and Mr. Selous were contracted to destroy whatever is massacring his herds. We have a duty to ensure the viability of his other locations, then we will seek out and kill that animal," Leon Roger said attempting to keep his composure.

"That being said, I believe then we have better odds with four men at arms instead of three. Miss Weaver?" Percival called out.

Jane turned to look at the five men standing a few yards away from her. Percival stepping over dead bodies and broken tree parts, shortened the distance so they could speak without yelling.

"Maybe you can assist us in hunting this thing. You said you have been tracking it for some time now?" Percival asked.

"Absolutely not," protested Leon Roger.

"I will contract her out with a part of my own share," Percival echoed towards the Captain.

His voice clearly making the point that this matter was not open for discussion and Leon Roger was not to debate him on it anymore.

"I agree. She is more familiar with this region and would be a valuable asset. If she knows its course then we need her help," Selous affirmed.

"I would feel much safer with four individuals protecting John and myself. If money is of concern, then I would be happy to secure Miss Weaver's wages to ensure our safety," Michael interjected.

"What do you say Miss Weaver?" asked Percival.

"I am in no need of takings. My only task is to find the Grootslang and kill it," she replied.

"It is settled then," Percival proclaimed.

"When we return to the compound be sure Jonkeer will be notified of this consortium with a foul heathen," Captain Roger roared with one last attempt at protest.

Selous moved quickly to catch up with Jane and Percival, Michael and John trailing only a few meters behind them. Captain Roger followed the group but purposely kept his distance.

John tugged on Michael's outer jacket signaling to hold a private conversation. He turned back to see if Leon Roger was within ear shot, the man was too far off in his own boiling rage to pay any attention to the two men.

"I feel we may be a little over our head here," John whispered.

"You wanted an adventure old friend. Here we are, ankle deep in the richest of adventures," Michael replied with a scheming smile.

"Our task is not to go off and hunt a killer elephant. We have a very specific job to accomplish," urged John.

"We have seen the fields of slaughtered slaves with our own eyes. They are taking us to another location that harbors more enslaved. Besides, would this Weaver women not be a fascinating exposition for your newspaper? I certainly have never heard of this infamous Haggar, but I am most curious to hear the tales. I am sure your readers would as well," Michael whispered with his head turned to prevent anyone from overhearing.

"These are dangerous grounds we are venturing into," John plainly stated.

"Relax old boy. Everything will go smoothly," Michael smiled back.

He increased his gait to catch up with the others, John stepped up his stride which turned into a small jog to follow.

IX

Monroe sat alone in a small hut. There were other structures all around the one he occupied. This area closest to the mansion was reserved for the slaves who worked in Gerlache's home. The other five members of the caravan were kept in similarly cramped quarters, though Monroe was not exactly sure where. They were kept separated, most likely, to avoid attempts at escape.

Earlier that morning Monroe saw the group leave for the fields through a separation in the boarded walls. Michael and John were accompanied by Captain Roger along with two white men he had never seen before.

The hut was poorly constructed with a bucket left in the corner for relieving himself. The rusted metal container was rarely emptied, and was full to the brim. When he first parted the Englishmen and was put into the care of Gerlache's slave masters, he was ordered to strip off his cloths and to replace them with a filthy tunic and even more disgusting pants. The ripped cotton material was stained with dried blood and possibly bodily excretions. When he first put them on, he wondered how many men were either beaten or died wearing these so-called cloths.

Holding the moldy piece of bread that was given to him as a daily ration, Monroe let the rancid feast fall to the dirt floor. He instantly felt a surge of regret knowing that there were many slaves all over the land who would kill for such a morsel.

Through the cracks in the hut he was able to observe and listen to the comings and goings of slaves and slave masters alike. Monroe was smart, well educated, and observant. During the early morning hours, he was able to pinpoint the ones he needed to watch out for and mentally calculated their routines.

Monroe patiently waited, biding his time for the prime moment to make his move.

The buildings that held the slaves were a hundred meters from the house, give or take. A short distance in theory, but the open space between the tightly packed sheds and the mansion meant that anyone attempting to clear the distance was vulnerable to being seen.

The slaves who worked the ground were kept in constant fear and terror, many willing to report on any wrong doing or mistakes for increased food rations or even a leniency in physical assaults. Monroe predicted that since they were of no threat of escape then there was a possibility the slave area was not under constant watch.

A loud ruckus was heard on the eastern side of his hut, towards the field. Monroe looked through an open knot in one of the boards in time to see two well-groomed slaves forcefully direct a large group of their mistreated brethren.

Monroe felt the moment was now, he bared his teeth and reached into his backside to remove a metallic tool he had hid away before they arrived. Relieved to have the hard object out of him, he moved over to the door and used the tool to pick the lock. Monroe knew he could just as well have kicked it open with his foot, but felt the noise and broken hinges would attract attention he had hoped to avoid. The game was stealth, the rules were all too familiar to him. There were risks you took when absolutely required but care and precision were necessary.

Making quick work of the door, he gently opened it and looked around to see if anyone had taken notice. When he left the hut, he closed the door behind him making sure it looked as if it were still locked. Holding his body tight to the outside wall, he took extra care not to make noise or to create a shadow that would draw the attention of any slaves packed in the surrounding huts.

Monroe kept low, slipping amongst the other structures, getting close to the edge of the collective. When he arrived safely at the last shed, he calculated the time it would take to reach the outer deck of the Chateaux. There were no railings, but plenty of furniture to conceal his presence, the problem for Monroe was getting inside. He thought about inching along to one of the side entrances, when an opportunity presented itself. He could barely see it but the window directly across from him was unlatched. Now the gamble for Monroe was, should he run the distance or make his way slowly across the wide space?

Both choices had advantages and risks. He decided a medium speed would be the wisest choice. Continuing low he moved with a swift pace across the plane, there was a slight step up onto the wooden boards of the outer deck. With his back bent, making himself smaller, he moved between one of the outer chairs and tables. Waiting here for a few seconds to see if his position was exposed, the atmosphere was quiet except for distant calls and a faint sound of cracking whips coming from the field. He moved in the shade created by the balcony above and in a crouched position pulled the window open.

He straightened his bent legs a little to look inside, the room was a small office, the door to the hallway was open leaving Monroe with another ideal opportunity. Pulling himself in, he bent down once again listening for any indication that he had been seen.

When he was confident that all was clear he pulled the window shut, then proceeded to move amongst the furniture using them to potentially block the view of anyone who might walk across the open doorway.

Monroe pressed his body against the wall with his arm barley touching the doorframe. The Chateaux was quiet, no footsteps could be heard, making Monroe think that the building was empty. In his head Monroe figured there were, at the very least, three slaves who worked primarily in the house at one time. He knew Leon Roger was no threat since he was in the field with Michael and Alan, but the other three men could possibly a danger to him. There was also Gerlache who could not currently be accounted for.

If there were slaves still in the house, they were possibly near the kitchen area, preparing Gerlache's midafternoon meal. The move was to find the stairs to the next floor and locate Jonkeer's office in the southwest corner.

Slipping into the hallway, to his relief Monroe could see that it ended at the base of a staircase. He moved with bare feet across the hall rug not making a sound. Grabbing hold of the banister he looked straight up toward the second-floor, step by step he traversed the incline with a pounding heart mentally preparing his actions if someone were to come into view. Even though he knew that the house slaves every couple of hours went to the surrounding camp to replenish supplies for the Chateaux, the stillness of the mansion was eerily distressing.

The growing fear of not knowing where Gerlache was created a hair-raising sensation on the back of his neck. Usually the man's booming voice could be heard from all over the building, including outside. Today was a most unpleasant exception, the man was nowhere to be heard. Monroe prayed that Gerlache had left for the afternoon on a business venture, because if he was caught by the Jonkheer it was not only his life he was risking but Michael and John's as well.

Making it safely to the second floor Monroe moved left to a cross section. He thought that the southwest corner was to the right of the connecting hall. Peaking over the edge of the wall he saw it ended at a large window. Crosswise to the left there were two doors at the far end with golden handles. Monroe eased down the long-carpeted corridor, he stood in front of the double doors and pressed his ear to the wood listening for anyone inside. He grabbed one of the golden knobs and pressed down, both doors popped open with ease, swinging into the room. Once inside Monroe quickly turned and pushed them closed making sure that they did not create a noise.

The room was huge. The wall of the office against the hallway was lined with bookcases neatly decorated with various bas reliefs and other tribal objects, ripped from their cultural origins.

Opposite the bookcases was a window facing the corner of the compound closest to the jungle, there was a large desk with an immense antique chair facing the office entrance.

Almost sprinting to the desk Monroe immediately rifled through the papers stacked on top. With the brief amount of time on hand he glanced over various notes by foreign dignitaries and property charters. He was hoping to find something concrete that would not be noticed if it went missing.

Monroe opened a few draws going through papers when he heard footsteps coming down the hall, he moved back towards the door holding himself against the bookcase left of the entrance. He could hear the doors to the room across from the office being opened. Further movement of the individual inside was unintelligible but after a few minutes the door was shut. The handle near him, after a few seconds, began to move, sweat dripped from Monroe's head, he paused, unsure of his next move.

The door swung open and in walked a decently trimmed slave, Monroe was curious as to what he was doing in the room and considered waiting to see. Instead, he acted on instinct and pushed the door shut when the man was halfway across the room. Before the slave could turn around Monroe chopped him with a straight arm across the side of his head.

It was a technique he was taught while serving the British, a close-range hand to hand combat tactic used when facing an unarmed opponent. The man began to fall and Monroe acting quickly, grabbed his torso before he was able to hit the floor which would have resulted in a loud, revealing thud.

Placing the unconscious body in the desk chair, Monroe now had to consider what to do with him. He thought about snapping the man's neck and disposing the body somehow, but was overcome with a surge of guilt. This man did nothing wrong and was a victim of a terrible atrocity, killing him would make Monroe no better than Gerlache or even Leon Roger.

Pressed for time, Monroe decided that the house slave had not seen him and that the man had entered Gerlache's private office probably without permission. There is a possibility the entire incident would go unreported. The slave would in no way risk telling anyone that he was attacked in a room he was not supposed to be in.

Monroe hoped the man would awake before he was found, or his punishment might ultimately result in his death.

Getting back to the task at hand, he continued searching the drawer left open before he was interrupted. There was a letter decorated with the royal Belgium seal, he knew enough of the language to decipher what was written and his eyes widened and heart paced with excitement.

It was a communique from King Leopold himself to Jonkeer Gerlache explaining that an Irishman, Charles Stokes, was arrested by forces in the Congo Free State for selling weapons to the Zanzibari army, located in the eastern region. The Irish had learned of the man's imminent court-martial. They were upset over Stoke's scheduled execution and were pressuring Parliament to open an investigation into the international incident. The reaction, by the English Government was to appoint a man named Roger Casement to probe into violations, by Belgium in the Congo, of the agreed upon accords established at the Berlin Conference. In reaction Leopold ordered the execution of all slaves in Gerlache's holdings and the disposal of any and all evidence before the British Consul could conclude their findings.

This information exhilarated and frightened Monroe at the same time. Obviously, Leopold was aware that the European nations were onto his dealings and that the threatened execution of Stokes was the catalyst they needed. It was curious to Monroe that Gerlache did not accede to his King's wishes, maybe the Jonkheer was not so eager to lose his comfy lifestyle in Africa.

Knowing he was now on borrowed time, Monroe anticipated that at any moment, someone would be looking for the man in the chair or even Gerlache himself would return. He folded the letter and hid it in the waistband of his pants then closed the drawer making his way to the door of the office.

Monroe opened the double doors and looked down the hall. With immense caution he followed the path he had taken earlier and found himself once again at the top of the large staircase.

With light feet he descended the stairs, halfway to the bottom a large heavyset man turned the corner, Monroe was now staring eye to eye with Jonkheer Gerlache.

Just a few steps above the Belgian, both men reacted with similar surprised expressions on their face.

"What is the meaning of this?" demanded Gerlache.

Monroe quickly spoke in a local tongue, knowing that a man like Gerlache would refuse to learn the language of his own slaves.

Feeling himself as a superior creature he would have no need to communicate in the dialect of those in a presumed lower station.

"You are the Englishman's valet. Your insolence will not go unpunished," Gerlache angrily barked.

Monroe jumped down to the step above the one where Gerlache stood, he then raised his leg and slammed the heel of his bare foot into the potbellied abdomen of Gerlache. The Jonkeer instantly fell backwards, tumbling to the bottom floor bellowing in horrendous pain. Monroe ran past him managing to get to the room with the window he had entered through. In his head, he organized his next move- to release the men and then go out to somehow find John and Michael. These tasks seemed impossible to Monroe. Deep in his nerves he knew the game was over and their lives were most likely forfeit.

Seconds before he was about to push the windows open the building violently shook, a loud noise like an explosion resonated from the other end of the Chateaux. Monroe was thrown off his feet away from the window. He attempted to stand up, but his head was woozy from the concussion and he fell directly against an open armoire that then toppled on top of him.

He would have been crushed by the collapsing ceiling above if it were not for the armoire that blocked the succession of wood, violently raining down.

He lost all sense of time and was unsure of how long he had been unconscious, Monroe awoke to blood forming around his face, pressed against the carpeted floor.

Turning to lie on his back, he stared up at the rear of the wardrobe, Monroe slammed his fist, with what little energy he had, against the cracked wood and continued until there was enough space to squeeze through.

The wooden tomb that encased him was severely damaged from the floor above collapsing upon it, making it slightly easier to break free. With gradual contorting of his body, Monroe was able to escape from the fallen support beams that crashed from the ceiling, as well as pieces of furniture that buried him in the chaotic rubble.

Once he was able to stand, blood began pouring down his face, his vision was blurry and Monroe realized that he had a broken nose and a dislocated shoulder. Wincing he grabbed the bridge of his nose and aligned it into place, letting out a bellowing cry of pain. He ripped off pieces of his clothing and shoved small sections of fabric into his nostrils to stop the bleeding, his eyesight began to clear allowing him to finally examine the damage to his immediate surroundings.

Being careful as he stepped over the wreckage, Monroe went through the door leading to the hallway.

Half of the wall was missing, sections of wood hung over the doorframe, miraculously the door was untouched. The entire

Chateau was in pieces, screaming could be heard from all over the grounds. Monroe walked into the hall, floor boards were now torn through the carpet with gaping holes revealing the dirt below the foundation.

The stairs had completely collapsed, a large section of the Chateau was missing. It appeared as if a giant bolder had been thrown directly through the structure, eradicating any and all in its path.

The cries of horror continued all around. Monroe looked at the bottom of what once was a grand staircase, a large patch of blood occupied the area where Gerlache had fallen.

'Did he escape?' he asked himself silently.

He made his way through the giant hole in the remaining wreckage of the Chateau and saw the slave quarters.

Some of the already destitute huts had been eviscerated, with bloodied bodies lying under splintered wood.

Otunba, one of the porters they hired for the journey ran up to him, he had a large gash in his upper brow.

"Was the compound attacked?" asked Monroe.

"I am not sure. The ground shook. There was yelling and all of a sudden a loud explosion," replied Otunba.

"Do you know if anyone saw what happened?"

"Heard a few men say darkness crashed through the building," explained Otunba

"Where are the others?" Monroe demanded.

"Everyone was able to escape. They gathered the carriage and are waiting by the east gate," said Otunba.

"Get the men to assist in freeing any survivors and take all who will follow to Lagos," ordered Monroe.

"What about the Jonkheer?" Otunba questioned, fearfully.

Monroe thought of the missing body and the blood at the bottom of the staircase's remains. If Gerlache was alive he was of no threat to them now.

"He is of no concern," assured Monroe turning away from Otunba.

"Where are you heading?"

"To help our men in the jungle," he yelled behind him.

Monroe reached the east gate before Otunba, it appeared as though their men were already helping the injured and freeing those imprisoned.

Their carriage was amongst a bunch of carts for fruit and other trading goods. He gathered his personal belongings, changing out of the ripped and bloodied rags. When removing his pants, the letter he recovered from Gerlache's office fell to the dirt. With all of the commotion he had completely forgotten about it, bending down to retrieve it he saw that drops of blood had stained the folded paper. He put the note into one of his cargo pockets for safe keeping. Monroe saw that his boots were misplaced so he put on an unfamiliar pair and grabbed his revolver.

For a moment he was distracted by the chaos around him, he looked up the hill in the direction of the wreckage. Otunba with some others were attempting to calm the survivors, groups started gathering in a cohesive formation. He smiled at the hope this sight gave him. Though these people had seen terrible treatment he wished them solace in Lagos. Monroe started towards the forest edge in the direction he knew Michael and John had gone.

As he got closer to the jungle there were deep impressions in the ground, bending down for a closer look he could clearly make out the tracks left behind. Monroe was not sure if these prints were just a coincidence, but following their path he could clearly see they led right up to the Chateaux.

He tried to reject the improbable conclusion, what the trail revealed had to be impossible. Monroe knew he should trust his instinct, but the idea that this destruction was caused by a large elephant was not rational.

The only relief came when Monroe realized that the imprints were heading away from the direction he was going. If what he suspected was true, there was a deranged animal out there and he hoped they would not cross paths in the near future.

X

Hours passed without a word spoken between the members of the party. Percival and Selous led in front as they passed through the jungle. Michael and John followed a few yards behind with Captain Roger in the rear. Jane Weaver was a dozen yards off to their left, coming in and out of their visual range. For most of the journey she kept in stride with the hunters, but every so often it felt as though she let her pace drag to keep a watchful eye on Leon Roger.

After their perilous confrontation in the field, combined with their currently grueling speed, the calluses building on the soles of John's feet began to burn. He, at one point, attempted to stop and remove his boot to sooth the throbbing pain, but was advised against it by Percival who explained that there were native insects that could get into the exposed boot and, if he were bitten, it would cause unbearable damage to his feet.

To John it felt as if the forest was getting hotter, sweat seeped into his eyes blurring his vision. He regarded how Percival and Selous effortlessly traversed the terrain. He admired how they never once showed weakness to the elements. John wondered if they were feeling the suffering elements as much as he was, perhaps their bodies were seasoned to absorb the infuriating heat, sharp scratches from branches reaching into their path, and dangerously angled rocks protruding from the ground.

Finally, the painful calluses caused John to miss a step. He fell forward catching himself before any serious damage was done to his face or legs. Pressing his body up off the ground, John checked himself over and looked at his hands to make sure there weren't any serious scratches. He recalled Monroe telling him to be mindful of all open wounds, what could be treated as a simple cut in London could be lethal out here in the middle of god's continent.

Percival and Selous paused simultaneously looking in his direction as John brushed himself off, this gave Michael a good enough cause to stop and lean against a thick tree truck to take a needed breath. Captain Roger continued his trek uncaring, walking past Michael and John then gaining ground ahead of Selous and Percival.

When he saw that the rest of the group was a good distance behind, he stopped and gave them a disapproving look.

"What is this nonsense? The day grows short, we have to make time," demanded Leon Roger.

"Perhaps we rest for a few. The events before were trying," replied Percival.

"We cannot afford the wasted measure," Leon Roger stated with growing aggravation.

"Then you go. We will catch up," quickly retorted Percival.

Captain Roger appeared as if he was about to continue on, he turned his head glancing forward. Rotating back to face the rest, John could see that a change in his expression revealed he thought better of it. A man like Captain Roger had the know how and ability to survive on his own in the jungle, but with the heat of the day quickly depleting his energy he understood the odds were dependent on the collective and going on his own could be lethal. There was also that raging animal! If there was to be collateral damage in their next encounter with it, Leon Roger felt one of the weaker of the group would be a perfect sacrifice to ensure his escape.

"Here son," Selous said taking out his canteen.

He walked over and gave Michael the container, who then took a large mouthful of water and passed it to John who took a similar helping before returning the canteen to Selous.

The refreshing cool taste eased the gritty dryness encasing their mouths and throat, Michael instantly felt a boost of energy. John looked around at their surroundings, the area was littered with huge chunks of rocks and boulders protruding from the ground. The trees around them were dense, the space between the trunks severely limited their perception of distance. At that moment John realized he hadn't seen Jane Weaver. He was sure he had seen her a short time ago but now she was no where in sight.

- - - -

Just because they couldn't see Jane didn't mean she couldn't see them. She sat on a rock a little less than a hundred yards from the group. The thick branches gave her a peripheral view of the others knowing that the leaves mixed with shadows from the forest canopy would take her out of their sight. Jane observed each man curiously, studying their mannerisms, attributes and physical traits.

The two large men who led the group as they walked were obviously seasoned hunters. One had previously mentioned being familiar with her and her father. Though she never met them before, there was an unspoken professional respect exchanged among the three. The other two men were from outside of Africa, Jane could tell this was their first time in the region by their gait and lack of preparation. She expected the one man to fall half an hour ago by the way he was landing his feet on the ground. He most likely had an abrasion on the bottom of his foot, she could only imagine how uncomfortable it had been for him. For the man following behind, it was without question who he was. Jane had instantly recognized Captain Leon Roger, formerly of the Force Publique. His pompous smirk, his gratuitous attire, only a man who places himself so high above the elements would wear an absurd outfit like that out here. Someone who considered themself immune to the dangers around him, his proud bearing spoke of the mindset the colonizers brought with them to this land. Jane felt deep in her blood and bones a rage for Leon Roger that would not be satisfied. Her core cried to her with a festering anger that the evil which was unleashed was due to the actions of this man and his ilk.

She removed a few pieces of dried meat from her bag, as well as her canteen, pulling off a small chunk with her teeth and then washing it down with a mouthful of water, she never once took her eyes off of the group.

The wind picked up, there was an immediate silence that washed over the forest putting Jane on high alert. An acrid stench occupied the area, she recognized the odor as that from the hole. Grabbing her rifle, Jane looked around diverting her attention from the others. She knew it was here, watching them, waiting for the perfect time to strike.

- - - -

John began to shake his foot feeling the prickly pain dissipate with the much-needed rest. The wind also picked up offering a cool relief to his burning skin. With the wind came an appalling smell. It was so pungent that the only word to describe it was offensive. He could see that Michael sensed the affronting stench, watching his friend's nostrils flair in an attempt to distinguish what it could be.

"The forest!" Selous spoke with an underlying tone of fear.

"The tranquility of advancing ruin," said Percival, turning around with a watchful gaze.

"What ruin?" asked Michael with a confused look.

"A while back I procured a contract to take wealthy American businessmen on a safari, I hired a hand from Chile for assistance. As we were traveling through the darkness, he elaborated that the truest fear in the jungle comes from silence. He recounted for me his survival from a volcanic eruption, Calbuco in southern Chile. Moments before the ground shook and the sky exploded the animals were quiet. The forest he was working in became unnaturally still. He called it *sonido de la muerte*: the sound of death."

The wind picked up blowing even stronger, every member of the group looked up at the sky expecting it to shatter down on top of them like from Percival's story, and it did.

A large tree, roots and all, dropped directly on top of them. The thick trunk crashed through the branches above slamming into the stony ground. John jumped to one side as the silence was broken by the thunderous impact, his foot got caught between two rocks as he made his jump to safety with a branch from the large tree slamming into his ankle. The hard bark sent a shock wave of pain through John's ankle resonating up his leg. He could feel the bone at his ankle break. The agony was so intense it over shadowed the affliction he previously felt on the soles of his feet. Selous ran for cover under the safety of branches on the closest tree with a large section of the falling limbs landing inches above his head. The sound of two heavy objects smacking into each other followed by the cracking of wood echoed overhead. Selous moved deeper into the forest away from the crash to avoid the oncoming breaking of the safety bough from above as it gave way to the heavy weight it carried.

Percival yanked Michael out of the way pushing the man from the falling danger, running for cover.

Jane witnessed the trouble first hand from a safe distance, she could not see where the tree came from just that it appeared to originate from somewhere north and directly aimed to land right on the group.

She saw that one of the strangers was injured and caught under the wreckage. Running to the man, she hooked both of her arms under his and pulled. He yelled out a huge scream of pain, Jane removed her arms out from under his and went over to observe his leg. His shin was, without question, fractured but luckily the bone had not pierced the skin; she knew that if it had this man would have been dead within hours. She observed his foot wedged between two rocks protruding out of the ground. Miraculously these rocks, which currently held his foot in place, were also the reason his ankle did not take the full weight of the tree's thick limb.

"Your foot is stuck. I need to move it slightly to dislodge it," she said to the man.

He was sweating from his brow and seemed to be in too much pain to comprehend what she had said. Jane thought there was not enough time to explain it to him again, she reached over the other side of the fallen branch and with both hands twisted his foot, pushing it free. The man yelled a ferocious roar of pain and passed out. For a brief moment she considered leaving him there to his fate but the sound of her father's voice muffled something in her head. She couldn't remember what it was but the comforting tone was enough to burn a fire of boldness in her veins. She grabbed the front of the man's jacket and began pulling him away from the fallen tree. Jane was able to get him over to the closest trunk and prop him up in a sitting position. Taking out a small bottle she opened the top and poured a little into one of her rags, then placed the rag over the man's mouth and nose. After a minute of breathing in the vapors his eyes shot open. Jane looked into his eyes with an aggressive look implying their next moves needed to be immediate action.

"Get your arm over me and move," she demanded.

Without question John threw his arm around the women and with a surprising strength she helped him get to his good leg. He kept his bad leg elevated with his foot dangling, keeping his toes above the ground. With every step he risked putting pressure on it, or having his foot bump into a raised rock which would coincide with a thrust of pain emitting from his ankle and making its way to his hip. She helped him get about a hundred meters away from the crash, then slowly placed him against a round boulder. Jane took her rifle off of her shoulder and held it in a defensive manner surveying their surroundings.

"I don't know what type of gratitude you are looking for, but I understand you could have left me to die back there," said John.

"Yes, I could have," Jane replied.

"I know the decision you had to make and greatly appreciate you saving my life."

"Our lives are not saved yet," Jane answered.

"I do not understand," John replied with confusion.

"It directed that tree to land on the group," Jane said.

"The fall was intentional?" asked John

"It was hurled," said Jane.

"I must be unbalanced. How could that have come to pass?"

Jane ignored the question, she looked in the direction of the tree and then behind her. Sniffing the air, she calculated their position and the safest distance to bring this injured man.

"We need to move. It will circle back around."

"I can not imagine I will be useful in a safe retreat. Leave me, I will call to my mates. They can not be too far along," replied John.

"You really are a stupid man," Jane said flatly.

John looked at her with an expression of hurt, he thought his plan was a noble gesture to relieve this woman of unneeded baggage and here she was insulting his brave proposal.

"How long do you think you would survive? A broken animal such as yourself wailing a hurt cry for help? If the vile monster hunting us does not find you, another hungry predator surely will."

Jane looked away from John, she put the strap of her rifle over her shoulder once again and kneeled down to his level.

"There is a ridge a short distance from here, we could make our way there and set up a safe camp for the night," said Jane.

"The night?" asked John.

"There are a few more hours of daylight on hand, we cannot waste them aimlessly looking for the rest of your group. We will set up camp, take care of your leg and get some rest. Tomorrow we will find a way to regroup with the others."

"Again, I find myself in your debt. Miss Weaver, is it?"

"Jane is quite appropriate."

"Jane, my name is John Alpert. Pleasure to make your acquaintance."

Jane helped John to his feet once more and they cautiously began making their way in the direction of the ridge.

"May I also ask what was on that rag you placed on my face?" John inquired.

"Lion pheromone," Jane replied.

"I would rather not know how that came into your possession," John said with a slight chuckle.

His last statement also brought a faint smirk to Jane's face. They continued the rest of their journey in silence.

- - - -

"Can you handle a weapon?"

Michael was still not fully aware of his surroundings, after the attack in the field and now almost being killed by a tree, his mind blurred in and out of reality. Everything felt as if it was being washed by a huge wave with a watery blanket drowning out all that was happening around him. The voice was muffled and he couldn't make out who was speaking, or where it was coming from. Michael never had such an impactful shock and it was completely overwhelming.

A hand grasped his shoulder and a gruff face eclipsed his blurry vision.

"Son, can you handle a weapon?" Percival demanded once again.

Michael looked the hunter dead in the face with a questioning gaze, he tried to answer but the words refused to come out of his mouth.

"Mr. Allen, I know this is a lot to take in all at once, but I need you to take this weapon and to be present," said Percival with a little more calming tone.

Michael grasped the handle of the pistol Percival was pressing into his palm, the variables of reality gradually came back into perspective for Michael and he began to pull in all his senses.

"I can handle a pistol," Michael replied.

"Good. We cannot survive with a stolid in our midst."

Percival stood up holding his rifle, he wiped his brow under the brim of his hat then turned to survey the area.

"Allan, where is our vantage point?" Percival called to the other hunter.

"Well Phillip we could go back and regroup with the others, if that felled tree hasn't killed them. We should not stay put because I believe that bull will come back around."

"Maybe we should double back," Percival recommended.

"I say that's a plan. I scouted a hill to our west earlier. We could go down it and back up the opposite ridge." replied Selous.

"What about John? We need to get back and find him." interjected Michael.

"Going back to the tree will leave us exposed. There might be predators circling the scene to scavenge," Percival explained.

Suddenly there was a loud scream and then silence.

"That was John. We need to go and help," Michael pleaded.

He quickly shot his head in the direction of the scream but was hit with a harsh dizzy spell and almost lost his balance, signaling he was going to keel over. Percival grabbed him and kept him on his feet.

"We will make our way back to find your friend but should not take the direct course, too dangerous," said Selous.

"My friend…," Michael began to protest.

"Your friend is favorably in the hands of Jane Weaver. Believe me, if he is in the care of her protection then he is safer than you are in the care of ours," Selous said cutting him off mid -sentence.

The group's attention was caught by the sound of something large moving through the forest a few hundred yards away, even Michael with his senses less attuned to such things, was aware of the movement.

"We need to abandon this position. I feel that this party is about to get a bit more crowded," said Percival.

The three men raised their weapons inching backwards as they kept their focus on the disturbance in the jungle. They retreated in the opposite direction heading west towards the direction Selous had recommended. Michael hated more than anything leaving John out there on his own, but if these men were right and this Jane Weaver was the legend, they made her out to be, then he was in good hands.

Well old boy, maybe we should keep this part of our tale out when we recant it for your sister, he thought to himself.

- - - -

Sitting with his back against a rock, John held in a growing scream that was building within his throat as Jane fashioned branches and vines around his ankle to set his break in place. The makeshift splint was basic, but would have to suffice out here where the nearest hospital was a few hundred kilometers away.

She took out her canteen and let him take as much water as he needed, then she removed some meat from her bag and gave it to him.

"What type is it?" asked John.

"Is that of real concern?" Jane clapped back.

It really wasn't, John thought.

He was starving and was sure once she told him what it was, his appetite would diminish along with his strength.

The light started to dim overhead and pretty soon it would be dark, he wondered if she would build a fire once the sun had fully set.

"Should we not build a fire?" John queried.

"No. A fire will attract unwanted attention. If you get cold, I can move you closer to some brush," Jane explained.

"Unwanted attention? Do you mean that bull from before?" John questioned.

"That was no bull," she answered with a cold anger in her voice.

"I heard you state that earlier," John noted hoping she would elaborate.

"It is a Grootslang," Jane voiced with the same anger.

"I am unfamiliar," said John.

"A creature from before the dawn of time." said Jane.

"A prehistoric creature? Like the bones Cope and Marsh are battling to find?" John pressed.

"I do not know of Cope and Marsh, but it came from before the lizards."

"I am confused. What exactly is a Grootslang?" asked John.

Jane sighed a little and removed her hat placing it next to her. She looked at John observing the curious expression on his face and decided to give in to his inquiry.

"When the earth was just water and rock the old gods created Africa at the heart of this world. There was nothing but stone, fire and a few scattered trees. The gods filled this land with various beasts, one being the Grootslang. This monster wreaked havoc on everything the gods of old created and they soon realized their creation was becoming too powerful and would soon be stronger than even the gods. The creators decided to rip these monsters apart and make two beings: the snake and the elephant. One to hold the power along with the intelligence, the other to hold its vicious nature and the malevolent hunger. There were stories told that the gods captured one deep in the bosom of the earth held in the tight grasp of Mother Africa."

"You think Africa released this primordial monster?" John asked with a rising fear.

"The land and her people have been offended and ravaged by the colonizers. Mother Africa's grasp has become weakened by the slavers, the monster has released itself." Jane stated with a venomous rage in her voice.

"Slavers!" John whispered to himself.

"Are you not a slaver?" Jane asked.

John did not know how to answer her question. This realization that the pretense he and Michael were engaged in to expose Gerlache, came in direct contrast with the reality he was currently facing. He was caught in a deep state of conflict: should he continue with the false narrative that he had been playing or reveal the truth to this woman who saved his life? The answer was easy but not simple.

"I am no slaver. I work for a publication in England, The Daily Guardian. The other man is my brother-in-law Michael Allen, he deals in commodity trades. We were tasked by the British government to procure evidence against Belgium in their illicit dealings here in the Congo," John admitted.

It felt good to finally reveal his true purpose here and to shake off the lie he had been living. The question facing him was: did this complete stranger believe him?

"It is such a wonder to me that men from far away come to this land, claim it as their own and then make agreements on pieces of paper that they expect others to abide by. The world is not small, despite the vain efforts of men such as yourself," Jane replied.

Once again John was at a loss for words, he constantly wrote and reported on the events occurring thousands of kilos away from his home. His readers knew nothing of Africa and its people, taking at face value that which they read in his paper. Yet, the "expert" who facilitated this information had never taken a single step on the continent, until now. Here he was deep in one of his own stories, yet he felt more lost and ignorant than if he were sitting at his desk reading telegram clippings.

His ankle burned. John attempted to move his leg in order to relieve himself of the discomfort. Jane went over to a bush and ripped off a few branches and leaves, she returned to John and put them under his calf propping up his injured leg. The slight elevation helped the burning heat radiating from his foot to his thigh. As he sat there in the forest, with the light gradually depleting, he wondered if his choices would have been different. With the ability to go back and warn himself of the approaching danger, would he ignore the caution and still head into the vast unknown?

The tales he would write, when he returned to London would be extraordinary. Finally he would have a first hand account of the darkest stories from within this mysterious continent. If they survive, he would expose the truth to those who claim to know the goings on and make recompense for his past fraudulence.

With this doomed thought lingering, John leaned his head back. He felt sleep was not wise but the spent energy and throbbing in his leg forced his eyes closed. He pushed off into a shadowy place of villains, heroes and monsters. Though in the waking world the ability to clearly identify the lines separating each was much more difficult than in the world of dreams.

- - - -

After the incident with the tree, Captain Leon Roger decided he had enough of this group and felt heading back to the compound was his best option. He moved through the forest with confidence and no real sense of danger. Having spent a lot of time traversing across Jonkheer Gerlache's land he was positive, even in the dark, that he would be able to make his heading. The only thing was that he usually had a small garrison of slaves with him for additional support, here he was alone with a maniacal elephant on the rampage. Taking a short rest, he relieved himself against a tree. Sensing movement up ahead he cautiously made way to a small hill and from the opposite side silently watched that savage woman, Weaver, giving assistance to one of the British businessman. Captain Roger was about to protest her assistance, as a guest of Jonkheer it was his obligation to see to the man's safety. His distrustful nature of the English called upon him to wait and observe. There was something off about those men, he was very loyal to Gerlache but sometimes Leon Roger felt the Jonkheer's judgement of character was mistaken. The European nations were closing in on Leopold's dealings in the Congo. Leon Roger as well as his other compatriots in the Force Publique, felt that there were spies attempting to infiltrate their operations.

He listened to them talking and overheard the wild women explain something about a demonic god from under the earth coming to wreak havoc against the outside infiltrators. Captain Roger felt a silent laughter rise inside of him in response to what he felt was utter nonsense. He wanted to save the man from further fouling of his head by this outrageous mystical folklore and superstition. Before he could intervene, the feral questioned the Englishman of his slave business, his curiosity pushed him to listen further and that is when the truth was revealed. At first Leon Roger presumed that the man was lying to her, but as their conversation progressed and the raw lie was fully exposed, the rage built up inside of him. The Captain knew that the British fellows were frauds, they were hear as spies, he now had the proof and would expose them.

Leon Roger prepared to sneak away and head back to the compound to reveal this deceit to Gerlache, but then he thought that this situation presented an opportunity. He would wait until it was fully dark and then kill Weaver, her presence was an insult to him as well as to the mandate of his people's destiny on the continent. After he disposed of the savage, he would then tie up and drag the man, John, back to the compound. Forcing this Britain to admit his trespassing by any means necessary, Leon Roger would then have him hung, along with his friend, in a tribunal. His execution would serve as warning to other European infiltrators of potential opposition to the Belgian Kingdom and to the rule of the King.

After a few hours he moved closer and saw that the Englishman was hard asleep. The woman was gone, this could be of concern but he saw that her belongings were missing as well. She could have left him on his own since he was maimed and served no purpose, he expected such a terrible and selfish act from an uncivilized denizen.

Captain Roger moved swiftly over the hill making sure to hide from sight, the two did not make a fire so his visual exposure was of no concern. As he inched closer to the sleeping man, Leon Roger unsheathed his knife. He moved on top of him and put the blade up to the man's throat. John's eyes shot open, seeing Captain Leon Roger menacingly above him holding a blade to his neck paralyzed John in a position of sheer terror.

"Do not move outlier," hissed Leon Roger.

John didn't say a word, his immediate thoughts were of his sister and Michael knowing he would die here and never see them again.

"You will be held accountable for your misdeeds against the Kingdom. I will see to it personally that you are hung...."

Before Captain Roger could finish his statement, a gunshot rang through the air bringing a look of surprise on both John and

Leon Roger's faces. Suddenly, a presence hung over both the men and a hard boot kicked the torso of Captain Roger off of John.

Jane stood over Leon Roger pointing a pistol at the man as he lay on his back in sheer astonishment. The Captain held his side and looked down at his hand as blood flowed from a wound punctured right over his ribs.

"How dare you steal a shot upon me. I should have expected a creature like you to shoot an unsuspecting man," Leon Roger coughed out with an immense amount of effort.

"Similar to putting a knife against a sleeping man's neck?" Jane answered coolly.

Captain Roger tried to reach his gun, but Jane quickly changed her aim and shot right at his hand. Leon Roger let out a scream holding his wounded hand now bleeding with a black hole right at its center. Jane reached down and grabbed his gun, she threw it far off to the side never breaking her locked gaze on Leon Roger.

She saw the strap form his rifle hanging across his shoulder, she gave the gun to John and took out her hunting knife. She placed the knife against the strap and cut through it with ease, pulling the rifle out from under him. Still holding his hand, with blood oozing from his side Captain Roger waited for the woman to come at him with the knife. Instead she bent down holding the tip of the blade right in front of his face.

"Now make way," ordered Jane.

Captain Roger looked at her questioningly. Jane straightened herself up and put her knife back in its holder looking down at him. Leon Roger first attempted to turn over, the pain from the bullet still lodged between his ribs exploding in his side. He put his good hand on the ground pushing himself up and was able to get one of his boot heels into the dirt getting into a crouching position. Against the pain building in his body and the aching in his hand he was able to stand, purposely leaning trying to relieve pressure from the side that was punctured by the bullet. He turned quickly giving the two, who were staring back at him, a departing glance. For a moment Captain Roger considered making a leap for his rifle. If he were to die, he might be able to take at least one of them out with him. He clenched his fist imagining he was holding the trigger guard of his rifle. His rage had clouded his judgement as it was his wounded hand and a sharp sting of agony moved from his palm to his elbow. The agony from his fist brought sense back into his head and he thought better of this fatal move.

Captain Leon Roger staggered away from them, he decided it would be best to get back to the Chateaux and get some medical help. In due time he would enact his revenge and kill them both, the man would hang but the woman: she would die by his hands.

- - - -

Michael and Percival sat by the fire waiting for Selous to return. After the incident, they made their way around the felled tree, traversing the rough terrain. When the emerging dark made travel difficult the three decided to rest near a large boulder. Selous said the vantage point was beneficial to them in case some brave predators crossed their path.

The hunter told Percival and Michael he would return and went on into the jungle, shortly after he emerged with a rag full of bloody meat. Michael watched with piercing eyes the mystery flesh skewer over the fire. When Selous handed him his portion he hesitantly sunk his teeth into the tough nourishment. It was far from the delicatessen he was accustomed to at home, but it was food. Michael silently reflected on how he missed Margaret's perfectly seasoned meals.

She was always fond of seeking out the newest cuisines from around the world, challenging herself (with the assistance of Nancy) to mimic the intricate recipes. Michael made a mental note that if he were to return home, he would sing her praise before and after every meal. The 'if' in his thoughts echoed over and over again creating a shivering unease in his body.

"What type of game is this?" asked Michael.

As the question left his lips, he felt regret inquiring where the meat came from. As he chewed Michael realized how overtaken with hunger he was, nothing short of discovering it was human flesh would stop him from devouring what remained in his hand.

"What did you do with the remainder?" asked Percival.

The other man took a large tear out of his meat washing it down with a mouthful from his flask.

"The carcass is hanging a good distance from here. Better to have the scavengers gorge themselves on a freshly laid meal than come foraging in our direction," replied Selous.

Percival grunted in agreement. The men finished their meal in silence, with the orange light from the fire illuminating their immediate area. The forest was full of chatter, squawking birds, whooping baboon calls and the occasional insect flying by their ears.

Percival took, from a pocket inside of his jacket, a small metal flask. He opened it and took a mouthful of its contents. Wiping his lips with the back of his hand he handed the flask to Selous who took a mouthful as well. Selous cleaned his mouth using a rag he had in his jacket.

Michael was handed the flask next and took a gulp equivalent to the other men, immediately wishing he had been a bit more reserved and cautious. He knew from the second the hot liquid touched his tongue that it was gin, but this was the strongest gin he had ever tasted. It burned a warm feeling from his mouth down his throat, settling in his stomach with a pound to his gut. Michael coughed a little and held back a retching feeling building in his torso, after the sensation passed a wave of satisfaction and ease quickly flashed over him.

"Easy boy, that is no Old Tom gin," said Percival.

"How did you come by that?" Selous curiously asked.

"Distilled it myself," Percival responded.

"That right?" Selous queried with a bit of surprise.

"I farmed Ostrich a few years back, lions came in and began hunting my flock. Was never much of a farmer but I became very capable at hunting. After a time, rich folk sought my services in gaming. A man from Schiedam contracted me for a week, he had Genever with him, a gin from South Holland. I told him I would take two days off my commission price for the recipe and he agreed. I did adjust his technique to give it a little more boot."

Percival expressed a wide grin following the latter then took another mouthful.

"That is fascinating. What about yourself Mr. Selous? What is there to say about you?" Michael asked.

"Not much to speak of. I served in Her Majesty's Army on the eastern front here in Africa. After a skirmish in the south I made a choice to stay. Fathered five children with two wives and contract my expertise just the same as Phillip," Selous responded.

"Nonsense. Novels of adventure and excitement will be written one day on our man's exploits. I have heard rumors he found a race of lost people and raided their stone temple of sacrificial gems, nearly being consumed by their crocodile god. The accounts of Allan Selous are as rich and deep as his pockets, do not allow him to be so humble," Percival boomed in response with a playful jibe.

"Is this the truth?" Michael asked with a childish curiosity.

He wasn't sure if it was the gin making him eager to hear more or the environment that encouraged the tales, Michael glanced back and forth from Percival to Selous with wanting.

"The facts are hidden in the fiction. I have had some marvelous encounters but let us not forget our friend here is also a renowned explore. His exploits are positively as impressive as my own," Selous replied modestly.

The men passed around the flask one more time, joking and being merry around the fire. The conversation moved easily, except Michael was anxiously awaiting them to inquire about his own life. Michael found himself with conflicting emotions, he had his fictional biography stamped in memory. After the brushes with death, he yearned for his wife, he desperately wanted to tell these men how he met his love, go into detail about her unconventional fascination with foreign foods and was most eager to tell her that he tasted panther and detail to her it's texture and taste. These men were just as privately reserved as their vague answers and never once asked Michael about his origins. Perhaps they just did not care, or more likely, with their characters, thought that if Michael did not offer his own story, he wished to keep it to himself. Percival and Selous did not appear to be men who shared. Though they shared a flask, a fire and meat, these two men wished to keep the dispensing of private matters as limited as possible.

Selous was the one to bring the jovial chatter to a halt and direct their attention once again to the matter at hand.

"I will take the first watch while you men get some rest. Michael you will take the second and Percival will anchor us into daylight. Are we in agreement?"

Both Percival and Michael nodded in approval as Selous removed his pistol and stood up to prepare for the duty of sentry. Michael rested back laying his head on the dirt floor of the forest, he watched the branches overhead sway in front of the thousands of stars that littered the sky. His thoughts raced as the stars and branches began to blur and he slipped into a hard sleep.

- - - -

Leon Roger made his way through the forest, the hole in his side throbbing with blood oozing down to his hip staining his pants. His surroundings were very dark, due to the pain he felt all over his body combined with blood loss, his vision was getting foggy. Captain Roger realized that his inability to accurately locate his position left his knowledge of the area unreliable. He would pause to rest against a tree and attempt to grab his bearings looking for familiar markers in order to give himself some sense of where he was. He looked up at the sky to locate the stars, the dense forest canopy blocked most of the heavens which, addition to his slipping faculty of sight, Captain Leon Roger for the first time in his existence questioned his own instincts. As a self-proclaimed predator of Africa, he knew if he didn't get on track soon, he was going to die.

Breathing heavily in the cooling night air, he was able to make out a steep dirt hill up ahead. Thinking that possibly reaching high ground give him a better line of sight to familiar territory, he made way to the base and attempted to climb. At full strength Captain Roger would have scaled the side of the hill within seconds, but his energy was waning fast and the bullet logged in his side prevented specific movements. A sudden motion in the wrong direction came with the risk of being shocked by a jolt of immense pain, resonating from his side working its way up his back. Planting his toes deep in the dirt he moved sideways, foot over foot up the hill gradually making his way. There were small trees halfway to the peak, Leon Roger, already feeling woozy and out of breath, grabbed for one to secure himself in place to rest for a moment. Unfortunately for him, in his fading state of mind he grabbed for it with his wounded hand. Captain Roger roared with agony, releasing his hand then falling backgrounds down the dirt hill. With each tumble he felt the constant concussion of pain as his legs rolled over his head arching his back and compressing the wound in his hand. His torso on the next rotating fall found the entire weight of his body slamming on to the same hand still throbbing from attempting to hold the tree.

At the bottom he landed on his side, the suffering with each impact on his wounds left no more exclamations of pain in him. In a semi fetal position, he stilled his body at the foot of the hill, surrounded by a thick black forest, alone and weak. Coming in and out of consciousness the fight in Leon Roger was not yet defeated. His mind attempted to will his body, in a last-ditch effort, to get himself up and moving. Even though internally he cried to his physical form to react he had suffered too much trauma, the blackness washed over him completely. After a time, Captain Roger opened his eyes to the dark forest surrounding him, unaware of how long he lay at the mercy of the jungle.

He rolled on his stomach and pressed his good hand firmly to the ground. Feeling the wet dirt under his palm, Leon Roger hoped that the floor was sopped with residue from a previous rain-fall and not his own blood. Bending his knees, Captain Roger was able to get into a kneeling position. Still mindful of his wounds, with careful maneuvering he was able to get to his feet. Now, the choice that lay before him, was should he challenge up the hill once more? It would most likely result in another fall leading to an even more crippling injury, so Leon Roger decided to make his way around it.

Pushing through the forest he blindly attempted to find a straight path. There were many large trees and thick brushes occupying the west side of the hill. It appeared to get steeper with large chunks of boulders decorating the boarder he was following, a stark contrast to the dirt slope he had fallen down earlier. This side without questions was more treacherous especially in his current condition. Deciding to abandon the thicket he moved further west to get clear of the flora that risked poking and stabbing his wounds. With an unsettling instinct Captain Roger was aware that the forest around him went completely silent. No calls to greet him, no nightly cries of an animal at the mercy of its mating rituals or being ravaged by a hunting predator. A man with his experience was instantly alerted to changes in his environment. He recognized the void of sound but needed to focus on more pressing matter. The only factors that were of concern to him were his current physical condition and the onset threat of impeding death that it presented.

As he moved around the thick trunk of a tall tree, a wave of putrid air rushed over him from above. The smell was toxic and revolting. Leon Roger looked behind and saw two red burning dots peering down atop of him. Before he could react, a thick muscular trunk grabbed hold of his body and began to wrap around his torso. With each breath he tried to take, the trunk squeezed tighter crushing his chest. Suddenly the bullet lodged in his side was the least of his pain, he could feel each coinciding rib cracking as the muscular appendage tightened its grasp on him.

He was lifted off the ground, the forest floor escaping from under his feet. The air temperature around him increased and with the burning air came the smell with an increased ferocity. Looking up to see his aggressor all he saw above him was a large gaping maw dripping thick froth.

The last image Captain Leon Roger of the Force Publique saw was the inside of the dark cavernous mouth he was thrust into, before the set of jaws lined with flat teeth clamped down shattering his head.

XI

Michael had a decent sleep considering the ground was hard and he was constantly rolling over a rock located near the small of his back. He stood up to see that Selous was nearly finished packing his gear, Percival had stood by for the remainder of the night watch which meant the man was possibly ready to go by the break of dawn. Michael, eager not to be the reason for delay and wanting to find John as soon as possible, dusted off the dirt that clung to his clothing.

"I think you forgot something," Percival said to him.

Michael looked around checking to see what step he might have missed in this unfamiliar morning routine. Percival pointed to the pistol he had side armed into the belt of his pants.

"Check your weapon."

Michael shook his head in agreement. He removed the pistol from his side then opened the cylinder, checking the frame and barrel for any obstructions that might cause him injury.

They moved on through the forest, Michael was lost but trusted the instincts of the hunters to lead the way. The forest began to thin out as they pressed on, hopefully heading in the direction that would result in Michael being reunited with a safe and healthy John. Michael sensed a raw, putrid fragrance in the air that intensified to the point that it was almost unbearable.

"You catch that?" asked Percival.

"Indeed. I do," replied Selous.

"I detected this odor moments before the tree fell on our group," Percival remarked.

A silent agreement passed through all three men. Selous looked up at a steep hill to the right of their path, there were a sparse number of trees at the top, and barely any bushes. Promptly, there was a crunching noise that appeared to resonate on the other side. Michel could see Percival take notice of the sound as well and look towards the hill on which Selous was focused.

"What is that?" Michael asked.

"Hush now. We must keep silent," Selous shot at him.

"It is the sound of bones being chewed," Percival whispered.

"I beg your pardon?" Michael said in a gagged astonishment.

"Selous take possession of my rifle. I am going to climb up there to see," Percival said in a strong whisper.

"What would be crunching on bones?" asked Michael insistently.

Neither Percival nor Selous answered him. Percival handed the other hunter his rifle then took out a hunting knife and carefully proceeded to the top of the hill. It was obvious to Michael that Percival was watchful about how he moved and where he landed his feet. There was no sound of his accession, it was only with his own eyes that Michael was able to tell the man was moving.

"What could be making that sound?" Michael questioned once again.

"It's likely a hyena or jackal. A predator like that could be dangerous if it is hungry enough. Better not to catch its attention, especially when it's eating," answered Selous.

Near the top of the hill, Percival dropped low and sprawled against the ground, inching his way up to the top. Once he got close enough, the hunter lifted his head propping his upper body up with one hand while still holding the knife with the other.

Both men at the bottom eagerly waited for him to give a sign, but Percival just stayed stationary staring off at the thing on the other side. Selous attempted to make hand gestures to catch his attention but could see his concentration was unbroken and frozen in either disbelief or fear.

"Follow each of my steps and do not falter even once," Selous ordered Michael, directly in his ear.

Michael nodded in agreement and carefully watched each and every move Selous made on his way up the hill, meticulously mimicking each stop and movement.

When they reached the position where Percival was perched both Michael and Selous raised themselves up to see what was on the other side. Immediately, they were stilled by the tremor of disbelief that grasped Percival.

The same creature from the rubber tree plantation was at the bottom, its tusks unnaturally longer and thicker than an average bull with veiny lines of indentations in them. The thick hide of the beast was black with deep cracks that gave off the appearance of scales, reptilian like.

The sight of the beast was not what shocked the three men, the offense came from what the monster at the bottom of the hill was feeding on, an elephant. By the size of the tusks it appeared to be a bull of medium age. Blood poured out from a wound in its head and the beast was chewing on the exposed ribs and inner meat of its bottom half. The sound of bones cracking and the slurping of meat was horrifying to begin with, but add in the fact that this elephant was being feasted on by one of its own kind and the sight was traumatizing.

Selous was able to break out of the spell of disbelief, he looked at Percival and grabbed the man's shoulder. The hunter turned his head quickly with an unblinking gaze and then regained his composure. Once Selous was able to bring Percival back he grabbed the back of Michael's jacket pulling him to give signal that they were heading down to their original position.

Selous quickly returned Percival's rifle and both men wasted no time in their retreat.

Doing their best to create distance from the smell as well as the sound, they followed the edge of the jungle to a stream. Michael had no idea if they were back in the direction from which they had come or even further from where they were going. Ever since their departure from the rubber field he lost his sense of direction and was unable to calculate where they were in relation to the compound.

"Either of you ever come across that in your journeys?" asked Michael between heavy gasps of breath.

Percival stopped short, he did not look at Michael or Selous. The hunter just appeared to stare off into the thick jungle, either contemplating the question or rethinking his strategy all together.

"A bull elephant consuming another. That has to be an odd sort of behavior," continued Michael.

"Indeed, it is unheard of. That was no elephant," Percival remarked turning his attention back to the men.

"It appeared to be one. I must admit my point of reference is limited," said Michael.

"In my years I have never come across one like that either," replied Selous.

"We need to find Weaver," Percival spoke if not to the others, more to himself.

- - - -

'That man almost slit my throat,' The thought repeated itself over and over in John's head. Three separate encounters placed him face to face with death in only a short period of time. For the remainder of the night he lay wide eyed and on high alert. Every movement was a shadowy figure with a blade or a monster with burning red eyes crashing out of the forest to tear him apart. John thought he felt fear before, but, this was something completely new to him, this was primal terror calling from deep inside. A level of awareness for the dangers surrounding John that he had never experienced before. This he supposed was where survival instincts collided with the desire to live. That thing that helped Jane Weaver and the other hunters make it through their tumultuous adventures.

At one point in the night Jane observed that John was awake and nowhere close to deep rest, his eyes darting back and forth. After searching through the dark forest for terrible unseen perils, his attention came back around to her. Jane and John's eyes locked in a silent understanding that these traumatic events had left a lasting effect on the untried mind of the Englishman.

"Tomorrow will be difficult for the both of us, especially without rest," she said attempting to reassure John.

"I cannot come to terms with these lethal chances," John replied with confusion and fear.

"He had been observing us for some time. The despot heard what you revealed to me," Jane admitted.

The latter sentence sent an icy chill over John's body. The realization that Captain Leon Roger knew the truth meant John and Michael had become political enemies to their host, and therefore, if caught, their lives would be forfeit.

That dangerous man was now heading back to the compound to reveal this information to Gerlache. For the first time since the incident with the tree, John's thoughts moved away from the well-being of Michael. His mind obsessed over the impossible task of somehow preventing Leon Roger from returning to Jonkheer's Chateaux and exposing his truth.

"He is still alive," John whispered to himself.

This dreadful thought passed through John's flesh raising small bumps on his arms, he no longer felt the aching pain in his ankle. He imagined each moment brought Captain Roger closer and closer to Gerlache, his vision became unbalanced and this dazed spell threatened to leave John on the brink of passing out.

"Not for long," Jane's voice was a force snapping John out of his dismay.

"Come again?" John asked with puzzlement in his voice.

"He will not make it far with the wounds I have inflicted upon him," Jane said with indifference.

After the encounter John was confused as to why Jane let Leon Roger live. He assumed it was an act of mercy, even though the Captain attempted to kill John in his sleep and possibly meant the same harm towards Jane.

He never got a chance to ask her why she allowed Leon Roger to escape from her gun. John was too absorbed in shock to process the question but once the thought resonated to the surface of his mind, he thought better not to broach the subject. John could tell that a woman like Jane Weaver was not accustomed to explaining herself to anyone.

From the way Percival and Selous regarded her reputation, as well as the way she handled herself in pressing matters, he understood that the respect afforded to her was well deserved regardless of the fact that her father was well renowned in the region.

Now he understood that it was not an act of mercy at all, far from it. Killing him right there and then would have been charity, letting him live was the true punishment.

Making way in the thick jungle at night with two debilitating injuries is a destiny far worse than that of a bullet to the head.

Bleeding out, unable to defend yourself against lethal predators lurking in the shadows, was horrible to imagine. A heavy burden was released from John's shoulders. He was unaware of it at first, but he was satisfied with the bleak outcome Captain Roger would face. His thoughts, once again, were on Michael and his safety. Only, after a few minutes of contemplating the fate of his friend, and the next couple of hours that would hopefully unite them, John started to feel a small sensation of guilt.

He weighed the emotion that his solace was based upon a man coming to terms with a horrible death, a man who would be unable to expose his secret. A small voice in the back of John's head attempted to reassure him that the man would see to the death of John and many others if he had made it back to safety. It said that this man has over his life time committed some horrible atrocities and that any demise he found in the jungle was far short of that which he ultimately deserved.

If not for Jane, then John would certainly have seen a similar demise. John didn't want to think about the creatures that would have found him pinned, with a broken ankle, under the large tree.

His thoughts were a montage of images, mouths full of teeth and claws. Blood spattered against a thick horizontal tree trunk, a vicious roar echoing in his ear. He wasn't sure if it was worse to preoccupy his thoughts with the brutal death of Captain Leon Roger, or his own potential slaughter.

The night aged and the darkness faded from black to gray. Jane stood up and prepped herself for the long day they were facing. She checked her guns to make sure they were in working order, then managed the supplies in her bag.

John saw Jane was up, and to not present himself as a burden moved to prove that he was able bodied enough to be self sufficient. The excess twisting from trying to lift his weight off the ground produced radiating pain. This was obviously a vain endeavor, as it was clear to both that John was incapable of moving without assistance.

"Stay still. Today will be demanding enough," she ordered.

When she handed him some of the dried meat as well as the canteen of water, John felt minute relief and did his best to pretend he was not completely helpless. The nourishment distracted him from the vulnerable feeling building inside. John ate every piece she gave him and made sure to take in as much water as he felt was appropriate with regards to their rations.

He held out the metal container in a gesture of return, Jane motioned back with a quick wave of one of her hands implying he was to keep the rest.

"There is a stream a short distance west of here. We will restock when we get there," she explained.

John shook his head in acknowledgement and drank the remaining water, savoring every drop that soothed the rough build up of dryness in his throat. As he held the empty canteen, wanting more, he promised himself that he would always appreciation the substance once he returned home where water was available in an obscene abundance.

John put away the empty metal canteen and saw that Jane was kneeling at his side. She was looking him over in a type of examination one would expect form a doctor preparing to do surgery.

"You comprehend what needs to be done?" she asked as if completing a conversation, they both started. He nodded in agreement, bracing for a slight infliction of pain that might come in the following seconds.

Jane aligned with his bad leg then John put his arm over her shoulder applying pressure to the area of her back between her shoulder blades. She put one of her arms under his injured leg and raised it slightly off the ground, with her other arm hooking John's waist she began to raise him slowly off the ground. John waited for a sharp ping that never came, he looked at Jane seeing she was meticulous in her calculated moves to get him off the ground. He at first was surprised at the attention she gave to helping him avoid any distressing motion but was also in awe at the strength she demonstrated in lifting him to his good leg. Jane moved slowly along with him acting as a bolster, to keep him balanced while preventing him from applying pressure to his injury.

John did his best to protect the injured foot from hitting obstacles sticking out of the ground. Jane held him up on the side of his bad leg and John found he was capable of stepping forward on his other leg with assistance from Jane. He mentally expected her to topple over immediately, but Jane held him with ease, fully supporting the weight John thrust upon her with each step he took. He could not believe the show of strength aiding a maimed man as well carrying their equipment.

The morning grew old and the humidity increased. As they steadily moved along, John contemplated what she said concerning the distance of the stream from where they had camped. He quickly concluded they both had drastically different ideas about the definition of "short."

John disliked the feeling of being such a burden to her and the impotence he felt towards himself. Twice the toe of his foot grazed a rock and the pain emanated from the center of his ankle through his entire leg. Both times John bit his tongue to hold a scream, he thought it would be in bad taste to complain about a minor inconvenience when the person beside him was carrying the responsibility of two people, literally, on her shoulders. The bright side (as he pointlessly tried to make a case to himself) was that his entire foot went numb after each strike giving him a momentary relief from the throbbing in his break.

They came into an area of the forest that thinned out just enough to see, in the distance, the far bend in the stream Jane had mentioned. As they closed in John could see that the water was murky. Back at home he would never entertain the though of drinking such muddy looking water but his lips were cracked and his throat was so dry that he felt as though there was a blazing desert tundra building in his neck and mouth.

From the moment he glimpsed the bend to when they reached the bank John counted the seconds over in his head, though it was quick it felt like hours at their current pace. Jane placed him on a large rock in the grass about a few meters from the stream. Placing her bags next to John she removed the strap of her rifle over her shoulder and cautiously put it up against the rock where he sat. He could tell she did not love the idea of leaving her rifle even if it was within a few arm's length. Jane then took out her side arm checking the bullets and placed it back into its holster, rummaging through her bag she removed her canteen.

"Take out your gun," she said to John motioning to the pistol at his side.

He looked at her quizzically, "Is it necessary?"

"Then you fill the canteen, and I will sit here to keep a look out," Jane replied.

John did not press any further and followed her instruction removing his revolver, placing the heavy metal on his good leg while holding the grip tightly.

She turned away from John, before heading toward the stream she carefully observed her surroundings, listening for any suspicious sounds. John could not help but find her reaction fascinating how she coolly replied to his reproach on her directions; she simply gave him an option that would be impossible to perform. Even when the question left his mouth a voice in the back of his head berated him for speaking it out loud.

She saved his life, twice, without protest carried him with safe passage, and of the two of them, was the only expert at traversing the land.

He silently promised to never question her, she had earned his trust completely and would hold that confidence as long as she remained by his side.

After she returned with the full canteen John took down three quarters of its contents immediately. When he was fully quenched John scolded himself for being thoughtless as to what was left for Jane. Jane showed no caring to the amount John drank. She finished the contents then returned to the stream to fill it up once more. She came back a second time and handed him the newly filled canteen and held it out for him, he shook his head, expressing gratitude but making it clear his ravaging thirst was satiated.

They rested for a time near the soft moving stream, the entire experience for John was surreal. He looked around and took in the environment, relishing the fact that he wanted nothing more than to be right here and to witness the land in its raw beauty. John only wished he could sit here and make notes about what he observed, the noises heard and the feeling of seeing Africa in all her glory. But John knew this was not ideal compared to his previous dreams. This was not how he had envisioned being on the continent when he worked and followed all the telegraph clippings from behind his desk. It was glorious, but the scenery held a lethality he was not aware of prior to this engagement.

John was without question a trespasser, an outsider in this land. Africa was showing him the grim reality that hid behind the exotic tales and exquisite sights.

Jane silently signaled it was time to set off by positioning herself close to John in order to help him up off the rock. John was struck by the urge to ask her where they were heading and how she knew what direction to take, but pushed back the impulse. He was not prepared to break the promise he had made to himself earlier. Once again, he had prompted his nature of inquiry to trust Jane Weaver completely, his intention was to put his fate in her hands.

They stopped abruptly standing perfectly still. John looked at Jane who lifted her chin sniffing the air. She turned her head appearing to find the source of the stench she detected. He looked at her trying to figure out what she sensed, there was a faint odor that passed his nostrils every time the wind blew strong but he was unfamiliar with it.

They moved along the water's edge going against the current. They had not gone a dozen yards when Jane immediately halted their progress, sniffing the air.

"Something is dead nearby."

John had no understanding how to react to this statement. Did she mean something human? Freshly dead? He could not sense anything different in the hot stale air but knew that her perception was more finely tuned to the environment.

She directed them along, following an invisible trail that only Jane could detect.

The putrid smell of decomposition wafted strongly into his face, holding back a gag reflex he now concurred mentally that there was a carcass somewhere within the vicinity.

A few more paces and John saw what appeared to be the body of a man on the ground up ahead.

A pool of blood collected around the upper half of the torso. The dirt floor of the forest was soaked with dark stains towards the lower half, creating a circle of blood around the deceased.

The clothing of the man was drenched in blood, as they got closer John could see that from the shoulders up the carcass was completely ripped off.

John could identify who it was by the outfit alone. The shoes, the pants, even the shirt caked with gore and blood, it was the body of Captain Leon Roger. A fitting finality of the previous night displayed right before them.

"Could it have been a cat?" John questioned.

"No claw marks. His chest had been crushed, then his head chewed off," Jane explained in a macabre type of nonchalance. Jane was pointing to the opening at the upper torso. "See the bones have been broken by flat teeth."

The stench of death was even more potent up close, John held back long enough and relieved the contents of his stomach. It was mostly clear bile, he was ashamed of himself for having such a weak stomach and wasting the precious water he had drunk earlier.

Jane with quick reflexes removed her pistol, did an about face away from the dead Captain Roger and pointed her weapon toward a cluster of trees.

"Come out or I will fire," Jane demanded with a loud roar.

A man stepped out from the shadows of the trees holding his own pistol aimed directly at Jane. John was surprised by the disheveled appearance of the man, at first the wounds on his face masked his identity but John soon realized it was Monroe.

"Put down Mr. Alpert or I will shoot," Monroe boomed with an equally commanding voice.

An excitement surged within John at the sight of Monroe. He felt as if a large weight was lifted off his shoulders knowing their compatriot was alive. This moment of relief was short lived when he came to the obvious conclusion that Jane and Monroe were within seconds of shooting each other, all in the name of his protection.

"Monroe, calm your aggression. I have survived many ordeals thanks to this woman," John reassured.

He moved his hand up to block the hypothetical bullet about to be fired from Monroe's pistol.

"Miss Weaver, this is the leader of our caravan Monroe Kelly. Monroe this is Jane Weaver."

"I am familiar with Miss Weaver and her exploits," Monroe spoke softening his tone.

He slowly motioned lowering his pistol giving Jane a suspicious look, waiting for her to do the same. Their eyes remained locked a few more seconds before Jane side armed her revolver and began assisting John closer to Monroe so that the men could have a proper handshake.

"Mr. Alpert, where is Mr. Allen?" Monroe queried with deep concern in his voice.

"We were attacked, our separation was sudden. I am hopeful he is with Mr. Percival, and Mr. Selous," John answered.

Monroe's eyes widened with a deep dread. "What was the nature of the attack?"

"A Grootslang," Jane interjected.

"I would normally question lapse in a logical explanation such as a Grootslang, but considering what I witnessed at the Chateaux…. I have no grounds to debate," Monroe stated while wiping the sweat from his brow.

"I have seen it with my own eyes. It is responsible for the death of an entire enslavement campo as well as the late Captain Leon Roger," John confirmed.

"Then the Captain will surely meet his man Gerlache in the seventh circle as the god's see fit," Monroe looked at John with a reassuring gesture. "I was able to procure the information needed for our mission."

"Let us then gather Michael that we may leave for Lagos," John spoke contentedly.

All appeared to fit quickly into place, John felt with Monroe and Jane leading the search they should promptly be able to locate Michael and the other men, then this dreadful experience would be closer to becoming a memory.

A loud roar echoed the surrounding forest. All three of their heads lifted in alignment searching for the source. Monroe in reaction removed his pistol, he pointed to a thicket of bushes and directed the group to retreat to them.

They swiftly crossed the area and made it to cover, the sharp points of branch ends creating hazards all around. John knelt on his good leg with the wounded one stretched out in front of him, a painful throb threatened discomfort but the fear of a monster within close range relieved any concerns; his heart pumping with-adrenaline laced terror numbing his mind to the injury.

Jane inched her way to the edge of the thicket opposite the side they had entered. In a crouching position she reached out pushing aside branches blocking her view. She peered out looking up towards the top of a distant rocky ridge. With the peak a little more than five hundred meters away, she could see the beast swaying its trunk and waving its massive tusks in the air. It looked so small at this distance but she knew that up close its size was considerable to that of an average bull elephant. Even from this distance Jane could see the blood and gore caked on the ivory of the beast's-fang like- protrusions. The Groostlang lifted up its front legs and slammed them into the ground bellowing another massive roar. Its lower lip flapped open spewing globs of coagulated blood each time it opened its maw to below another siren call into the forest.

Jane reached out to tap Monroe on the shoulder, when she caught his attention she pointed in the direction of the ridge. Monroe turned his body and leaned forward to the opening Jane created with her hand. With wide eyes he witnessed the dark mass sitting on top of the rocky highland. For the first time he witnessed the behemoth that almost took his life, a living legend right out of the darkest reaches of Africa, free to ravage unhindered.

Its black eyes were clearly visible to Jane's piercing vision and she could almost make out, in the black pools, the pinpoint circles of red in the center.

Jane looked at the astonished face of Monroe. It was clear as day by the expression on his face that all doubts about the existence of the monster were washed away

"Its presence is a bad sign," Monroe whispered.

Jane glared at the beast and pulled the rim of her hat down over her eyes to break her line of sight. She could not watch it any longer afraid it would become an obsession leaving the group exposed to the possibility of drawing its attention.

Jane nodded in agreement with Monroe. Her mind weighed down with heavy consideration of the task at hand. Though its presence was a small piece of a larger problem, she knew she had to take care of. The release of the Grootslang had to be addressed immediately. The seal to the old gods had been broken, now she was faced with one of their most grievous mistakes.

Jane spoke with her regular volume, "It must be destroyed."

XII

The hat on Michael's head did little to protect him from the blistering heat raining down on them. An earlier image still burned deep within his mind. Michael Allen considered himself a pragmatic man who lived for reason and science. He would listen to experts and take their word above any religious zealot or superstitious peddler, but he was sure more than anything that what he saw was a monster. There was no scientist nor psychologist alive who could successfully convince him otherwise. Michael was positive the thing eating the elephant was not of this world, and by the looks on the faces of the 'great white' hunters, he believed they reasoned the same.

"You hear that? There is a stream up ahead," Percival called back.

The gruff man's words broke Michael's daydreaming spell that was cast by the wake from shock. He looked around trying to listen and focus but to Michael every sound was foreign and new. Fear had gripped him tightly, his nerves were wound into a

pressure knot with every sound and movement posing as a potential danger.

Moving out of the dense forest they came to a grassy patch
with pockets of tall grass growing off the bank of the stream, small
bushes broke from the grass at random intervals. Michael knelt by
the brown water with his knees sinking into the muddy shore that
lined it. He dipped his hand in and splashed the cool refreshing
liquid on his face, instantly soothing his burning skin. Gratified,
he was given,finally, a moment to catch his breath, relieving the
tension building inside. Kneeling on the bank, with is hands on
his bent knees, Michael observed, with deep admiration, the
blurry reflection of the sun on the stream's surface.

A rough hand grabbed his shoulder, Michael looked up to
see Selous blocking out the bright light from the sun. The combination of shade and glare from the orange glow emanating from
behind the silhouette, blocked the man's face. Selous moved to
the side giving Michael a clearer view of his features and from
that angle he could see there was a concerned look on the hunter's face.

"You alright son?" asked Selous.

Michael had no idea how to answer. Of course, he was not
alright, he was an unfathomable distance from his home, had lost
his best friend, and there was a monster somewhere in this jungle
potentially hunting them. There was nothing alright about any of
this. He also knew this was no time to lick his emotional wounds,

if John was in trouble then sitting by and feeling sorry for himself was not going to help him.

"I will be. I believe," Michael replied feigning a brave smile.

"That's good to hear. Organize your composure and let's get a move on. Don't forget to fill your canteen, never know when we will come upon another source of water."

"Glad you haven't gone all nutty on us. Nothing like an irrational companion to make a bad situation worse," called Percival who stood up from filling his own canteen.

Both men enjoyed a good chuckle on the comment and even though it might have been at Michael's expense he joined in, good naturedly. A smile was rare now and it was no use ignoring a moment to wear one. He dipped his canteen into the murky water filling it halfway, then lifted it to his mouth taking a few mouthfuls returning it into the stream to fill the rest.

Michael felt a little better, the men at his side would have his back as long as he showed them that he would have theirs. The situation was not ideal but there was no point in making assumptions that could make it any worse, he just had to hope.

'Marvelous things were accomplished with hope,' Margaret would say.

Standing up he stretched his legs and looked down stream to see how far he could spot its path. Michael imagined that it would eventually lead to a large river basin that even further on would make its way to one of the coasts.

There was tall grass even further down, trees leaning over the stream casting shade. He cleared his eyes with his pointer finger and thumb convinced that what he saw next was a mirage. A big hulking mass with its head bent down beyond the trees was looking directly at them, its tusks stained red and black eyes, as clear as day, filled with an impenetrable rage.

A large hand grabbed the back of Michael's jacket pulling him back around the opposite direction. A hard forward push instantly signaled his brain and legs that it was time to run. Michael did not turn back to witness the creature thrust its massive body across the stream, exploding water and mud hurtling into the air. If, by chance, he had turned his head and saw the speed and ferocity with which the monster was moving towards them, it would have deadened his nerve and courage, possibly sealing his fate.

The men ran back into the thick forest from which they had come, jumping over large overhanging rocks and coming close to impacting with large trees that were blocking their straight path. Michael did his best to keep an eye on any dangers that formed in front of him as well as keeping peripheral sight on both Selous and Percival. His survival function was switched on and some of his movements and reactions were involuntary, giving Michael an inner astonishment. He was breathing heavily, lungs burning, legs pleading to quit but the fuel of fear ran deep within. Michael perceived the events as if he were looking out of a window in his head, not in control, with someone else directing his body

Branches thrashed against their faces, tugging at their clothing, threatening to reduce their speed or trip them into a lethal fall, resulting in the large monster pouncing on them instantaneously.

Without the need to look back, Michael could envision it battering through the foliage with an unrelenting rage aimed at the three. There was an immense heat of abomination radiating against his back. In his mind he pictured the large evil thing from beyond, morphing into a huge wall of fire burning through the forest.

After what felt like kilometers of running the forest opened into a large grassy plane. The grass reached up to their knees and within a few meters from exiting the forest edge the ground dropped into a large crack. They paused at the edge observing the trench before them. It was about a dozen meters across with steep clay walls dropping down three or four meters to a brown and orange dirt floor. Michael hesitated then witnessed Selous and Percival slide down the walls of the depression into the earth, his reflexes, quickly called into action, following their lead.

"Watch your step son! This sinkhole could be unstable," Selous yelled out to Michael between heavy gasps of breath.

Michael had no idea what a sinkhole was. He had heard about perilous tales in foreign lands where adventurers came upon dangerous regions riddled with sinkholes, but he always assumed they were made up by the author or story teller to make the narration more thrilling.

Michael made it a point to follow the depressions in the ground created by Selous' steps who was just a few paces ahead of him. His mind reverted away from the fact that there was a monster chasing after them. He imagined when he returned home, he would romanticize to party goers, recounting how they fell into a sinkhole with a behemoth chasing them.

Then the memory of the black-eyed beast resurfaced crashing him back into reality with the pulsing fear reengaged him.

They ran the length of the trench to the far end, the top of the broken earth with grass protruding over the orange clay wall a couple meters over Percival's head, just out of reach. Michael caught up to the men standing by the obstacle before them. Percival looking directly at Michael bent his knees interlocking his hands.

"Quick man, I will give you a lift, grab the edge," he ordered.

Michael placed one of his boots into the pocket made by Percival's locked hands. With a quick thrust he was given a boost by the man's full strength. Michael reached up towards the rim but could not quite grasp the ground above and fell back down almost landing on his back.

Luckily Selous was right behind him preventing a hard topple, immediately straightening him to his feet. Percival gave Michael an urgent look directing him to attempt the act once again. The hunter's eyes said enough, there was no time to waste, the monster would be on them any second and it was imperative that he reach the earth above.

Michael stepped into Percival's hands one more time. With this try he extended his leg into a jump for an extra launch out of the hunter's boost, the trick worked giving Michael a bit more height. His hand reached the ledge and held on, his fingers digging into the soil above trying to push down for leverage only to discover was that the broken ground was soft earth. Michael's hands sunk into the grass over the brown clay, the dirt underneath started to crumble when Michael attempted to lift himself up. The soil and grassy layer breaking apart sending him falling back down into the sinkhole. The descent felt much longer, the black mass of the beast could be felt nearby and Michael understood that was their last effort. Selous and Percival were not prepared to catch him, understanding the futility in another attempt, they took their rifles off their shoulders and braced them ready to fire. Michael landed on his back, the clay soil creating a soft impact. The wind was knocked out of him and Michael stood as he labored for breath. He turned his gaze to the other end of the crack, the Grootslang hovered over the edge looking down at the men with burning black eyes. Michael who was closer to it now than he had ever had hoped for, could see pin point red dots in the center. At an elevated height it materialized even more into an unnatural beast. He considered old teachings from his time as a choir boy "this much be hellmouth" he thought, as fear constricted deeper in.

The creature lifted its massive trunk, swaying its head in a display of anger. Michael felt a sense of relief for a moment thinking they may be safe in the dirt crack, the beast may be unwilling to pursue them. His moment of reprieve was short lived. Before he was able to express his concept to the other men the Grootslang moved forward. The hulking body lurched down laying its front legs on the steep dirt wall, its massive body slid to the clay floor, breaking apart fountains of clay and dirt to spill behind it. Instinctively, Michael took out his pistol and began to fire, most of his bullets struck the wall of the sinkhole behind the creature, but one did strike its shoulder creating a bloody hole in the scaly black skin.

The monster roared with even more rage than it held before and started to charge them.

"There now, you have gone and angered him," Percival called sarcastically.

Michael could sense an attempt at humor by the man's voice but no one was in the mood to create further commentary. If the consequence of Michael's hit on the beast expedited the ensuing pursuit, then they were obviously no better off than they were before.

The legs of the monster pounded into the ground, its feet depressing far into soft floor. Michael thought he felt the earth shake beneath them with each leap it took towards the men.

He knew that any moment it would be on them. There was a sense of eager anticipation for the other men to release an array of bullets, hoping that one would strike the beast with a miraculous blow, dropping it dead.

Percival and Selous held their fingers pressed firmly against each trigger of their rifles, delaying until the beast closed its distance. There was a single thought running through their minds, 'If they were going to die, then they were going to put a lethal amount of hot metal into the monster beforehand.'

The black eyes came into view, Percival felt that he had a clear shot and just before he pulled the trigger, seconds to the moment it was upon them, the ground beneath the Grootslang gave way and the monster was swallowed into the earth.

Michael was perplexed, at first it looked as if its hind legs became stuck. Then the floor around the creature fell into itself giving the clay soil a liquid appearance. In seconds the monster's hind legs then body disappeared, followed by its roaring head until only the thick muscular trunk swayed out of the earth and slid into the ground like a thick black snake.

All three were paralyzed, they stared at the spot, where it was engorged, with eyes of disbelief.

"Aye, you were right Allan, this be a bit unstable," Percival quipped between heavy gasps for air.

Michael looked at the man with astonishment, he would have to compliment Percival, later, on his atypical humor.

"Well, when we get out of here, maybe one of you gentleman could clarify exactly what a sinkhole is," Michael interjected with his own brand of jest.

The three looked at each other and all shared a good chuckle, brief chortles released between their attempts to catch their breaths. Looking around Michael considered that they were still stuck in the depression, and even though their last attempt to escape was futile their next attempt would not include a giant monster.

"Any ideas on how we could get out of here?" Michael asked.

He turned to see that Selous was already working on their exit strategy, the hunter proceeded to tie a line of rope tightly to the hilt of his knife. Selous then put his hands out motioning Percival and Michael to make way, he started to swing the rope in a tight circle with the weight of the knife as a balance. Michael was not sure how Selous understood the correct speed of the rope and knife's rotation but with an internal prompt the man ceased the movement and in full motion the knife was pitched up over the edge. Though it landed far out of sight and all that was visible was the rope leading above them, onto the unbroken ground, it was clear the blade landed perfectly as planned. Selous then gave a quick heave to secure the cutter's position, another tug on the rope proved that it was secure and that the line would not give way.

Selous turned to Michael handing him the rope, "This you will find as a handy assist with getting over the unstable rim."

Percival for the third time bent down in position with his hands together, Michael grasped the rope tense in his hand. He was lifted up by Percival and like the attempt prior gave himself a boost up with a bounce from his leg. As he ascended Michael released one of his hands from the rope and reached up to a section of the line laying on the grass near the broken earth, he held his grip half expecting the tautness of the umbilical to give way, but much to his surprise it stayed true and Michael found himself securely suspended above the ground and the men below. He wanted to look down but quickly kept his mind on the task and hand over hand pulled himself up over the lip of the sinkhole back onto the safe grassy foundation.

Selous boosted Percival next who then in turn with help from Michael pulled Selous out of the depression.

When all were out and feeling the subsiding of the heart pounding fray they had just experienced, Selous moved over to the knife embedded into the grass flooring, and dislodged it. He then untied the rope from the hilt and placed the knife back in his belt and the rope in one of his cargo pockets. None of them was too eager to continue, they all looked at each other with appreciation for their survival then, as if called upon by some silent whisper, they simultaneously turned their heads back towards the rim of the sinkhole. Shoulder to shoulder all three men moved carefully towards the broken ground and peered into the large trench. They were looking directly at the location where the Earth swallowed the Grootslang. It appeared completely unblemished, if it were not for the large tracks leading up to the spot, the men would not have been able to tell there once was a monster giving pursuit.

"What is the prospect it survived?" asked Michael hesitantly.

"No man would have survived," said Selous putting emphasis on the word *man*.

Michael turned to the hunter understanding what he was inferring, "You are insinuating better to assume it is still alive?"

"Safer not assume at all about that creature. Especially that it is dead," Percival replied while removing his hat to clear sweat from his brow.

Percival looked at the gun in Michael's belt, "Let me see that pistol."

Michael glanced down at the weapon momentarily forgetting it was even there. He pulled the pistol out feeling the weight in his hand, observing it with wonder and fear. He was pretty sure that he struck the beast but the monster was unfazed. Michael wondered what use the weapon was if it did not hold the power to stop the creature. Focusing on the details of the gun he understood that, though its stopping power might have been futile against the behemoth it did make him feel safer. He looked at Percival still waiting for the handover and realized he had been peering at the revolver longer then intended. Michael passed the pistol to the hunter who then performed his own inspection. Percival opened the cylinder and dumped out the empty cartridges from the rounds Michael had fired. He reached into one of his pockets removing fresh bullets then filled the now empty chambers. Percival then clicked the cylinder back into place, pulled the hammer ready for discharge and handed the weapon to Michael.

"When the time comes, make them all count," he said to Michael with a cheery grin.

Selous was the one to break the moment of content with harsh reality, "We should move with haste. If that thing is alive, I would rather not be present when it gets clear."

All three nodded in agreement and turned away from the sinkhole. Once again, Michael felt himself unsure for where they were going and questioning whether he would see John again. Fear returned like an old friend, but not one that paralyzed, it was more a fear that ignited. There was something inside him burning to answer the questions he desperately sought, and driving him towards finding his lost brother and making sure that they both left this continent together, in one piece.

XIII

The storm was an unwelcome addition to their list of misfortunes. John was surprised and startled at how quickly the sky had darkened, then instantaneously came a sky shattering clap of thunder. The rumbling appeared to be a wake-up call for the oceanic level of rain thrashing down upon them. Even in London where they take pride in their efforts against wet conditions, John never thought that he would find a land that would shadow the levels of precipitation he experienced at home.

Monroe yelled something incomprehensible towards Jane who was only a couple of meters ahead, the noise of heavy rainfall drowned out his voice. Just minutes before they were hit with the downpour both Monroe and Jane took turns aiding John, though it did not go without a little debate. From the behavior Monroe was displaying he assumed their man took John's current situation to heart, and possibly blamed himself for the predicament. Though it was preposterous, in John's view, to think that there was anything Monroe could have done to prevent what had unfolded with the tree. John himself felt deep relief that Monroe survived and since their reunion expressed this to him more than once. Monroe expounded upon his risky maneuver at Gerlache's Chateaux. How he discovered the letter from King Leopold of the genocide planned for the entire enslaved population, to his heart pounding encounter with the Jonkheer on the stairs, then within seconds of the entire operation being laid bare the building was trampled by an unseen force which they all agreed was most likely their menacing pursuer.

Whenever Jane observed Monroe struggling with John and requiring a break, she would offer assistance which Monroe would reject in a protective manner. John would, in order to quell the situation, recommend taking a few moments rest to give Monroe a break and then, when their pause was over, offering his arm to Jane, hoping that he was not insulting his man by undermining his position but displaying for Monroe a show of trust towards Jane.

Though the rain muted any coherent words, Jane heard his call and acknowledged Monroe. In response, she pointed toward the opposite end of the grassy field where they could barely see the edge of the jungle. The distance might have appeared more than manageable in ideal conditions, but because of inclement weather and John's pace they were far from that state, which made the stretch feel longer than it should have been.

John was drenched, the rim of his hat protected his face but he could feel his boots and jacket getting heavier as he moved. As they made way, John found his movement hindered and lightly pulled back by Monroe, he looked down and saw the man's foot had gotten momentarily caught in a patch of mud. It took two strong pulls by Monroe to release his boot and they continued. Jane, eager to check ahead for danger, was already close to the forest edge. She was just a blurry image against a backdrop of a dark, obscure jungle. Monroe and John began to close their distance to her. As they approached, John could see that Jane remained stationary, holding her position before entering the jungle. She held her rifle in a ready position and it was clear she was scouting the immediate interior. Monroe, feeling the tiring aches of heavily drenched clothing, accompanied by the weight of another man, did not wait for her. He pushed forward with John at his side into the dark, canopied wild.

The flora ceiling of the jungle provided protection from most of the rain but small spirts of water drizzled through openings creating sections of miniature waterfalls. The dark gray sky already made visibility difficult but inside the jungle there was almost no light and John had a hard time seeing which direction they were going. Moving deeper into the gradually darkening jungle they found a rock protruding from the roots of a large tree, Monroe sat John down and took a deep breath.

The light around them was minimal, rain still drizzled down atop them but it was a pleasant reduction from what they had just experienced. The thunderous pounding from the rain was muted. John could hear the sound of rain hitting the leaves above but it was not as bad as the painful level of noise out in the field.

Jane made her way to meet both men, still holding her rifle in a defensive manner. No one spoke, John felt the urge to say something but every time the words reached his tongue he held back in reservation. He felt a pang of despair. The rain would make finding Michael and the others even more difficult. John wanted to ask what their next steps would be and to reiterate the fact that there was a monster possibly stalking them. So many things could have been said out loud but with each thought John realized that the numerous glairing realities were obvious to all of them. Bringing up their current tribulations would only increase the fog of doom that hung over them, though when John looked at Jane, he felt a surge of confidence, a fragment of hope splintered his dejected thoughts.

She stood close by, looking around with a strong posture of confidence. If the woman felt fear, John could not imagine she ever showed it. Jane Weaver was a stark image against the bleak and wet forest backdrop. Once again, throughout their travels, he secretly said a prayer of gratitude that she was at his side, as if the land sent an emissary to shelter him from the forces at work.

John gained the confidence to speak and break the silence, "Monroe, are you familiar with the Grootstlang?"

"I have heard many things on this land. Stories that would come off quite odd to outsiders, but fit perfectly into the fabric of Africa," Monroe explained "I was working with a spice trader out east. There is an island with pockets of madness rumored to be spreading. We made our way to the town of Tanga where one of my contacts was supposed to collect cargo. One night we were drinking spirits at an establishment when there were cries outside. We went out to find a crowd of people gathering around a man who…" Monroe reached up with a gesture to touch his face then brought his hand back down, a blank stare washed over his expression.

He continued, "There was chatter amongst the men, they kept referring to a demon bat that was spreading a disease."

Monroe sat quietly for a moment. John could see in his eyes, he was reliving the experience and just from his face alone it appeared utterly horrifying.

"The image of that man's body burning that night will forever haunt me. His face… his face is indescribable," Monroe whispered his voice trailing off.

Jane was facing away from the men looking towards the darker section of the forest, but when Monroe spoke the name of the town in his story, she turned giving them her profile.

"You said Tanga?" Jane asked with strong curiosity.

Monroe nodded in response, Jane averted her eyes towards the forest once again in contemplation. Both men looked at her feeling she had more to add to the subject but instead she turned away.

Jane stood up and began to walk, getting close to the location from which they had entered the forest. The landscape out in the field was faded by the continuing rain. Jane focused her vision keeping an eye for any movement. Far in the distance a black blur moved across the field, Jane knew immediately. Any casual observe would brush it off as an elephant. The movement of the thing out in the field was that of a predator, it was that of a creature hunting.

Jane quickly returned to the men, putting an arm under John's, "It is not far off in the field. We must head deeper in."

The thought of going deeper into that blackened forest struck another wave of fear in John, but then the image of that thing out there making its way towards them punctured his nerves even deeper.

As they moved into thicker jungle, the blackness around them grew, diminishing their already impaired sight. John's good leg became heavier with every step, the water collected in his boot combined with the thick mud on the forest floor made his knee ache and burnt the muscles in his calf with every step. The only thing pushing him forward was the thought of that thing, driving a wave of energy into his veins, giving him just a little more each time he wanted to quit.

His bad foot struck a rock, a loud yell escaped involuntarily from the depths of his lungs. The group stopped at the sound, no one moved or spoke listening to the forest to see if the noise gave away their position. John could not see Jane clearly but heard her shuffling through her bag off to his right, suddenly there was a small explosive light. He could see that Jane held what was probably the remains of a lucifer match and was lighting a sheet ripped from a larger rag. Jane held one end of the rag up high, away from her body, the burning end hanging down to give them some light. Looking around as the sheet quickly burned away, she pointed off to a large tree ahead.

"Appears to be a clearing. We can make our way there to regroup," she whispered.

The fire reached her hand and Jane let go of the remaining cloth which lit up in the air, then the ashy remnant floated down. John, once again finding himself in complete darkness, felt the strength of Monroe giving him assistance. He tried to lift his foot even higher than before to avoid another impact, his leg and hip surging with what felt like a thousand thorns coursing through his blood; his muscles turned to rock.

John assumed they reached the tree because Monroe removed his arm out from under his own propping him up against what felt like a thick tree trunk with irregular bark.

Moving past the tree Jane could see much better than either man in this level of darkness. Her senses were heightened and she opened herself to any input from her eyes, focusing also on the senses of her nose and ears. There was nothing, it was strange to her how empty this part of the forest felt. In her experience, even in the blackest part of the forest, there would be some sign of life or movement, but this place felt like a void. It reminded her of the open rock she came upon at the bottom of the hole.

She took out another match and lit another shredded piece of rag, raising it up and away from her body she took in the view with astonishment.

Before her was an opening, a circular field guarded by an ancient looking trees and a ceiling of thick branches, their leaves creating a tight nit roof blocking out any light. The ground was a graveyard, dead bodies and appendages covered the floor.

From what she could see they were mostly those of elephants, all in different stages of decomposition. Jane looked closer and saw there was the randomly placed body of a few men among those of the dead beasts.

Their hunting uniforms told a tale of poor saps who possibly ventured off into a region not meant to be seen by those from the mortal world, who would never live to tell the tale.

A strong wind blew through the void, the fire reached Janes fingers and she released the remnants of the rag which extinguished into burning embers that immediately went out once they hit the ground.

A low growl reverberated through the air, appearing to come from their right side. Looking in the direction of the sound Jane could see small pin sized red circles. The Grootslang was here, Jane dropped down quickly squeezing her body between the decomposed torso of a medium sized elephant and a more recently dead one. She could hear the hulking mass of the monster move slowly in her direction. Making as little sound as possibly Jane pressed herself into the decomposed carcass hoping to utilize the exposed rib cage and hardened skin to block her from the monster's sight. Lying on her back, she tried to adjust her eyes to the dark, looking between two rib columns she could see the creature was holding something with its trunk dragging it along the ground to its side. The Grootslang made its way to the tree that she recalled Monroe and John were hiding behind, she suspected it had not seen them or her as of yet or they would all have been dead by now. The monster lifted the thing it was holding and dropped it against the roots of the tree. It began to lumber away when it stopped short, lifting its trunk, it moved the muscular appendage raised in the air, as if it was tasting the atmosphere. The creature swayed its head giving Jane a perfect view of its side profile, at that moment she was almost sure it saw her. Jane froze in a deadlocked stare, seeing its black eye with the small red mark in its center. The beast did not move, just stood there, then after a moment it continued on and exited the area from the direction in which it had come. Jane stayed in position, laying in the carcass. There was no question in her mind, she understood positively that it saw her. So many unanswered questions swarmed through her head until her thoughts were broken by sharp whispers.

"Weaver?" Monroe called as quietly as he could.

Pulling herself out from inside of the elephant carcass, she raised herself into a squatting position. Monroe walked over close enough for her to see the outline of a look of relief on his face.

"That was very close," he said.

"Maybe so," she replied, thoroughly replaying the events in her head.

She moved over to the tree where the creature dropped its carry, lighting another stripped piece of rag she brought it up to reveal the body of a man.

Monroe knew instantly it was that of Max Gerlache, still wearing the gold sash he sported when Monroe gave him a kick in the gut.

The corpses' white suit was stained with blood and one side of his head was caved in, Monroe could not help but feel that this was a suitable end for such a vile man.

They collected John, the three decide to head in the opposite direction from where the beast was headed.

As they moved further from the monster's lair, light slowly came back. At first John could see objects further away than before, then details revealed themselves followed by colorful objects such as a flower on a vine. The canvass of darkness was being pulled back, revealing the jungle. John imagined that the area from which they had emerged was a hollow hole in the land that sucked all inside creating a cavity, devoid of light.

With the return of light, the forest grew thin revealing the sky and sounds from the rain which continued but with less intensity. When the expanse of forest was completely visible Monroe and Jane surveyed their immediate surroundings while John sat resting on a sloping tree trunk. They both went in opposite directions agreeing to move no more than a hundred meters from the tree on which John sat.

Monroe was the first to come back from his reconnaissance, "There is a clearing west, that leads up to a ridge. We can circle back and possibly find our party there."

"I cannot be sure I will have the energy for that," John said with uncertainty.

"Do not lose hope yet Mr. Alpert. This is not the place to fall into despair," Monroe said while looking around to see if Jane returned.

"We cannot aimlessly permit ourselves to be corralled by this thing until it kills us," John urged.

Jane's voice come off from an unidentifiable direction., "I feel that is exactly what it is doing."

Her presence startled both men equally.

"'Can you elaborate on that thought Miss Weaver?" Monroe inquired with a slight hint of anger in his voice.

"It is herding us," Jane said flatly.

"Then what shall be our next course?" John interjected.

Jane turned away from the men studying the area as she spoke, "If one finds themselves hunted, you do not allow the predator to direct you. We get it out in the open, lead it in the direction we desire instead of being pushed by its whim."

"What direction?" Monroe asked sounding like he was accepting this plan.

"There is a valley towards the North. We make our way there," Jane said turning back to look at Monroe and John.

"I must admit I agree with your presumption Miss Weaver but my responsibility is for Mr. Alan and Mr. Alpert. I must consider their well-being before all," Monroe turned towards John "I say Mr. Albert we head back to the compound grounds. I will be able to gather men there to retrieve Mr. Alan with you safely secured."

Monroe's tone was insistent but also, for the first time since John had met the man, he could hear a pang of doubt in his voice. John understood that what Monroe proposed was the most logical path, but he also knew by all he saw that this was no logical situation.

Jane was curt, "You will be dead before you reach your destination."

John felt the truth of her statement stab him in the heart, by the look on Monroe's face the wound was inflicted deep within him as well. This monster was unpredictable and was no mindless beast. It was cunning and they needed to plan and act taking into account its intelligence and malice.

"I cannot leave without Michael, Monroe," it was the first thought that came to John's mind following Jane's blunt statement.

"As you wish Mr. Alpert. Lead us Miss Weaver."

John knew that Monroe needed prompting from him to follow Jane's charge. The man knew what she said was truth and understood her expertise should be trusted, but to Monroe his duty to John and Michael was of the utmost importance but to a fault that sometimes could lead astray from rational thinking.

Monroe assisted John off the tree and they proceeded in the direction in which Jane led them. Her path was straight forward and it was clear that she knew precisely where they were headed and how they were going to get there. A grey wall of rain and mist became more visible behind the trees ahead revealing to John that they were, once again, getting closer to exiting the jungle. As they got closer to the clearing John could see that the gray had hints of blue and yellow sunlight stretched behind it revealing that the rain was giving way. Drops of water still dripped down from the canopy above but the appearance of sunlight was a warm welcome, perhaps a foreshadowing of events to come, a good omen, John secretly hoped.

Standing on the fringe of the jungle looking across a hilly grass field they could see the base of a forested mountain. Their elevation gave them a fantastic view of the entire area, once again he was amazed by the scenery before him and saddened that due to circumstances, he could not enjoy it for the splendor it was. Behind the highland were even larger ranges whose summits were blanketed with clouds in the sky.

Jane began to move toward the peak, Monroe began to step with John to follow and suddenly the Englishman's confidence waned when the prospect of trekking up its incline became more imminent.

"If it is anywhere in the area, we will be spotted the moment we step into that field," said Monroe.

"You take John, I will keep watch and be on the defensive," said Jane, never breaking eye contact with the opposite forest.

Jane rechecked her rifle and pistol making sure they were fully stocked. Monroe made sure he had a good grasp on John and mentally prepared for the hard trek they would be making to the other side.

Monroe could feel the hesitation in John's movement, "Are you ready Mr. Alpert?"

"Makes no difference now does it Monroe," John spoke more of a statement than a question.

The clouds broke apart in the sky revealing the full force of the sun. The emerald grassland rolled up and down ahead of them in dips and peaks making it look as if it were moving, like an illusionary green ocean with its waves crashing into the foot of the mountain ahead. They were voyagers against the plane that could leave them exposed to treacherous hazards lurking under its serene front.

- - - -

Michael was the first to see the muddy depression, he almost fell straight into it which would have been a perilous end to his journey. It was close to eight meters deep, not a lethal drop but the clay mud at the bottom appeared thick and sopping from the rain, it would without question have sucked him into a suffocating casket of earth. Like the sinkhole earlier, Michael had read stories about quick sand and quick mud from adventure novels. In nearly all the tales, the hero gets caught and is miraculously saved by a low hanging tree branch or a compatriot who coincidentally comes through at the last second to aid the protagonist. Looking down into the pit it was clear to Michael that there would have been no rescue. Once one fell down there, a person would be taken by the viscous matter, never to be released. The walls of the hole looked very unstable. Even if he didn't sink immediately there would have been no chance of climbing out. This would be the final resting place for any poor soul who descended unknowingly, to its bottom.

Selous and Percival flanked Michael on either side. Percival knew that sinkholes, mud quagmires and other perilous topography were common in Africa, but to happen upon a depression like this a short distance from the other fracture in the earth was curious to say the least. Percival stretched his arm out in front of

Michael's torso, encouraging him to step back from the edge in case there was a give way.

The forest was thin here and luckily for them the rain had ended. Protection from the forest canopy above would have been unhelpful because of the prior storm.

Selous looked around and observed the ground of their immediate surroundings. There were chunks of mud and clay scattered all over with large stains of orange colored mixed with darker shades encompassing the hole.

He motioned towards the brown chunks that caked the grass and rocks, "It appears something has broken out from here."

"I don't see a need to question what that might have been," Percival said with a gruff voice.

Selous tracked a path of the orange mud clay mixture trailing away from the depression, he could see vividly prints pressed into the ground. They were unclear, possibly due to the heavy rain, making them indistinctive. A seasoned tracker like Selous could tell there was a trail but it was hard to estimate in which direction it went.

Selous pointed toward a direction he decided upon by an educated guess, "It might have gone in that direction. I recommend we double back and…"

Blood spewed from the hunter's mouth spraying over Percival's hat and hitting Michael's jacket. A large cone of ivory broke through his chest, cracked pieces of ribs breaking to either side and blood dripping down his abdomen. For a fraction of a second Michael and Percival were frozen in shock as they watched Selous' body raise a few feet off the ground. From behind him emerged the monster with its angry black eyes and scaly skin still caked with small patches of orange clay. Selous held on to his life for only a second or two more before his chin and body went completely limp as he hung impaled on the menacing ivory tusk.

Percival snapped quickly back into the moment, raising his rifle at the beast's face, half shielded by the dead body of Selous, and began to fire, striking it right above the left eye.

The Grootslang raised its front legs with a load roar, thrashing its head from side to side. The body of Selous lifelessly swayed along until the violent movement dislodged the hunter sending the corpse sailing through the air until it collided with a tree then dropped to the ground as if it were a bloody hunk of meat.

Witnessing a dead Selous being tossed about jolted Michael into action. He removed his pistol and shot off two quick shots. Like before, they were aimless and missed their target. Michael pulled back his arm holding the gun and mused over what Percival had said earlier. Raising the gun again in a more confident stance he took aim preparing not to miss, as he fixed his gaze on the target. The Grootslang, free of the corpse of Selous, bowed its hulking head with the two large fangs protruding from its face, making as if it were preparing to charge.

Percival grabbed the jacket of a focused Michael and screamed in his face, "Run, boy!"

Without further encouragement he dropped his arm holding the pistol to his side and ran with Percival right behind him. Just like before, the feeling of a big dark goliath pursuing them was brooding over them from behind.

- - - -

Jane, Monroe and John had reached the edge of the forest, at the base of the mountain, when they heard the sound of shots echo across the open plane.

They remained stationary right at the borderland listening further Jane was pretty confident that the sounds came from the area of the jungle to the west of the range but second guessed her estimation. Uncertainty rose amongst them, Monroe knew what Jane was thinking and that their next moves could have drastic consequences if they were not careful. The shots could have originated from another skirmish that did not involve them, therefore it was prudent that they create distance to avoid the aggression. There was also the possibility that the Force Publique discovered the destruction at Gerlache's compound and were on the offense to find the perpetrators, or even other antagonist group that would without question put Monroe in shackles and do god knows what to Jane and John.

The seconds ticked by, there were no further sounds of discharged firearms but a decision had to be made. Monroe was considering over his choices when running out of the jungle, from the far western trees, came two men at full speed. Monroe and Jane both saw the small figures emerge and then swooped at a diagonal towards them, Jane held her rifle ready to fire and Monroe grasped the grip of his pistol with the same mindset.

John was the first to actually identify the men, "Hold back!"

John was relieved at the image of Michael alive, a swell of emotion built inside of him. Tears began to accumulate in the corner of his eyes, John pushed back the need to break out into a weeping fit of joy.

Monroe saw that it was Michael running with another man, he did not know his name but by the looks of him deduced it was possibly one of the hunter escorts that Gerlache had sent with Michael and John days before. Both men appeared disheveled and filthy, Jane observed the blood drenched across the front of Percival's jacket.

Still over a hundred meters away, Michael yelled at the group, "Behind us!"

Suddenly Jane and Monroe were on guard once again. Michael ran up to John putting his hand on the opposite arm that Monroe currently had slung over his shoulders. Michael looked his brother-in-law over, there was much to discuss and elaborate on but there was no time at all for familiarities.

Michael removed his hand from John's arm and placed his hand behind John's head preparing for a warm embrace, they were about to hug when both men shook their heads in a tender nod. The acceptance and appreciation for being alive was exchanged silently between them, the time to act, to continue that survival, was now.

Michael grabbed the opposing arm Monroe was holding, he looked at their liaison in a grateful manner but also dictating that he would be assisting John. Monroe, thankful for the reprieve gave Michael a gesture of thanks.

Percival stood in front of the group and turned around looking like a man who had accepted his fate and was going to show no quarter to their pursuer, he was not prepared to run anymore. The death of Selous shook him and to continue retreating from his murderer would be an act of cowardice and dishonor to his fallen comrade.

The five of them stood in front of the jungle which remained stagnant, the intense building of anticipation waiting for the monster to emerge became almost unbearable to all. When, after a time, it did not present itself, it was obvious the thing was nowhere to be found.

"This is curious," Percival blurted out.

"I agree, we should double back across the field," Monroe urged.

"NO. The Groostlang is directing our path. We cannot bend, we must press forward," Jane called out to the entire group.

"I am not sure I can go back into the forest. What that... thing did to Selous is..." Michael trailed off his final words obviously trying to push the image of Selous' impaled body out of his mind.

"Behind us is nothing but death," John sighed looking at Michael apologetically.

Percival surveyed the grassland, "If we stay out in the open, we will be able to see an ambush."

Silence washed over all of them like an old friend, each personally licking their mental wounds and conserving energy for the next move.

Jane herself dreaded the fact that remaining out in the open was a dangerous and frightening proposition, but going back into the forest allowed the Grootslang to control the situation.

Michael and John looked at each other with a toxic mixture of shared fright, the desire to go home, and the urgency to forget this failed adventure they had embarked upon.

Jane broached a radical plan, "I believe this field runs parallel to the valley west of here. If we head north and cut across to intersect with the river, we should find commerce vessels. They will give us passage."

Before anyone could consider their objections or acceptance to the idea, a roar blasted from the south. There was no illusion as to where the sound came from and all of them turned and to look toward the offending direction. The vast grassland hooked around the jungle that Monroe, John and Jane had emerged from. The sound appeared to originate from an area where the two forests opposite the open land appeared to merge near the peak end of the field.

It was already past midday with the sun beating down on them hard, when John found himself secretly praying for rain.

Percival pointed towards the area, "Miss Weaver, that be the direction of the river?"

She shook her head understanding the gravity of such a long distance and was hoping that the hunter was not inferring what she suspected.

Percival with regret in his voice acknowledged John, "The man is a risk."

Monroe and Michael were about to angrily object to any-thing Percival said further but Jane immediately responded in a calm, demanding voice.

"Each of us is a peril to the other. The impact of leaving someone behind would incur a heavier toll than if we took a maimed with us."

"The only cost of leaving him behind is that to our soul," Percival retorted.

"That is too high a cost to HER. We cannot predict how SHE will react to such an act of aggression," Jane said never breaking eye contact from Percival.

Percival wanted to protest further, but Jane's word stung his mind. That single phrase repeated in his head, the others may not have known who she was referring to but Percival, being on this land for such a long time, recognized the living essence that surrounded them. Jane was talking about Africa, and to lose her favor, at a time when there was little to go around, was unwise.

Percival thought out loud, "Who am I to question the judgement of a Weaver?"

XIV

The forest was business as usual, life around them was teaming with chatter and untamed energy. Despite the dark cloud hovering over their existence, the group moved deeper into the jungle. Every moment was an anticipated effort to keep going, knowing that the evil lurking in the shadows could be steps away. Their passage was slow, it was understood there was no point in rushing, especially with an injured man in their company.

The sun moved across the jungle ceiling. After hours of walking, the sun hidden behind the northern mountain, the light fading significantly in the thick flora. Soon visibility would make travel perilous and they would need to camp for the night, there was no point in aimlessly traveling in the rich dark.

There was a brief discussion on whether they should build a fire or not, it was agreed upon that the Grootslang possibly knew where they were regardless, a fiery blaze would not dissuade it from attacking them when it desired.

Around the warm glow of the burning wood they all kept to themselves. Percival was cleaning his weapons, and checking his supplies, Jane sharpened her knife and cut some dried flesh off of snake meat she kept in her bag, and Monroe folded and unfolded the paper he had absconded with from Gerlache's office, looking like a man second guessing every decision he made up to this point.

Michael sat next to John, together they watched the logs burning, illuminating the jungle night around them. Usually there was much to say between the two men, but at this moment both were at a loss for words. Each had his own experience, a need to share the horrors they went through but also wanting to protect the other from the nightmares they held. There was no point in recounting the terrors they witnessed aloud. How could pressing the burden of such dangers on a loved one help them make it through the experience? Both men quietly promised themselves that they would one day openly discuss what occurred when they were safely sitting in Michael's study far from the worrying ears of Margaret

"I insist when we get back you stay with Margaret and I for a time," said Michael.

"I cannot become a burden on your household. Being one here is enough of a weight on my shoulders," John protested.

"You would be no such burden. We could use a nan once there are children in the house," Michael answered turning to his friend with a curt smile.

"The better, I would not be a burden but a chambermaid," chuckled John.

"I could find you suitable attire old boy," Michael laughed back.

The tension was broken, they felt their rightful routine fall back into place. It was a comfort for John to have Michael by his side and Michael felt the same.

John looked at his longtime friend and placed a hand on Michael's knee squeezing, "We will endure this."

"All the more reason I want you around. I will not abandon you once again," Michael said with a desperate expression.

"Is that what you feel? You abandoned me? My dear friend, such feelings are undeserved. I feel just as beholden to you. There is no imbalance in our duty to each other. We are on equal grounds," John said attempting to reassure Michael.

Michael leaned back looking around at the others.

"Yet you are the one who will leave with the scars," Michael said with deep regret regarding his friend's injury.

"We will all leave with scars Michael. The emotional injuries you and the others hold are just as significant as the one on my leg," John said.

Monroe stood up and walked over to the two Englishmen, he bent down and looked at the wrappings around John's ankle.

"You men should get some sleep. The three of us will keep watch during the night," Monroe insisted.

"We should leave at first light," Percival called to them, overhearing Monroe's comment.

Michael decided it was time to speak about the yet unspoken, "Are we not going to discuss this monster?"

"What is there to discuss?" asked Percival.

"Is there a means to kill it? Can it be killed?" Michael pleaded.

"It can be killed," Jane replied.

"We saw our bullets pierce its hide. Though they had no effect on slowing it," said Percival.

"Why does it kill elephants?" asked John, "That lair was full of carcasses."

"I can only guess the rage it feels for the elephants, a reminder of what the old gods did to the rest of its kind. The others which once ruled the land amongst it," Jane elaborated.

The night came, yet no one slept. Michael and John lay against a tree trunk shoulder to shoulder watching the fire burn. Percival would sit for a few moments then get up and move to another location, his inability to quell his angst created a tension in the atmosphere. The man who appeared very self-assured and calm looked like a caged animal now. Jane was the only one who seemed to be resting. She sat against a large root protruding from the ground, pulled the brim of her hat down over her face and did not move. John looked at her, wondering how she was able to remain unafraid, or, at least able to conceal her fear so well. He supposed that everyone displays fear by various means but Jane was capable of accepting the fate at hand. She always allowed the situation to unwind in front of her, instead of permitting the uncertainty to eat her from the inside. He guessed that was the key, to put faith in the fact that nothing was truly in their control, they were at the whim of some outside force.

Monroe, officially on first watch, saw Percival's distress. He went over to the hunter who was now sitting, Monroe squatted in front of him.

"This man Selous, was he a close friend of yours?" Monroe asked sympathetically.

Percival looked up at Monroe, not with anger but curiosity, as if he was unsure how to answer the question.

"No," Percival answered directly.

Monroe treaded carefully now with further inquiry, "His death left a deep impression on you though?"

"I have witnessed many men meet their fate in the jungle. Our profession is full of lethal choices, out here anything can draw you into the end game. Years ago, a man I was contracted with was ripped apart by a vicious group of Hyenas. There were five of us on the safari, the animals were only three in number. Their desperation must have run deep to come at us. They grabbed him and pulled him into the shadows, I remember hearing his screams as their teeth ripped him open," Percival explained not making eye contact with Monroe.

"This loss is different," Monroe stated.

"It was a part of the order, they were trying to survive. The Hyena's fear of death overpowered their fear of us. That thing that killed Selous killed with malice, no fear in its eyes, there was nothing just emptiness. Its actions held no desperation, no need to survive just hate and anger. I have never seen any animal do that before."

"It changes the fabric of things," said Monroe.

Percival turned his eyes to meet Monroe's, "That it has. If I am to make it out alive, my time in the jungle is finished."

"What would you do?" asked Monroe feeling that Percival was burning to answer.

"When I saw the tusk break through Selous you know what my thought was?" Percival asked.

Monroe shook his head slightly feeling that the question was more rhetorical than literal.

"I thought of ostriches," Percival answered.

Monroe tilted his head in a questioning look, "Ostriches?"

"Before I took up the mantel of the 'great white hunter' I use to farm ostriches. It was very peaceful. Witnessing Selous die, I feel, was a call to return to the farm."

Monroe stayed crouching in front of Percival who diverted his eyes to look down towards the ground. Possibly staring off into a different world where he was back on the farm with his ostriches, far away from the current horror.

Monroe decided to let the man be, he stood up leaving the hunter to contemplate life and his choices, alone and in peace.

John, who wasn't aware he had fallen asleep, suddenly he found himself cast into a dream of disorganized thoughts. A misaligned world where the jungle met London, sitting at a table with Monroe, Margaret and Michael. In a cloudy vision he looks up at the wall in a building that was somehow that of Margaret and John's home and Gerlache's compound all at once. There before him was the head of the Grootslang, stuffed and presented as a prize they had won, its black eyes still burning with the red dot in the center.

Everyone was at the table talking, John could not look away from the gruesome trophy when the snake like trunk extended out towards him and opened wide like a mouth. As John was being eaten whole, he screamed for the others, who just carried on with their conversation, oblivious to what was happening. In the snake's mouth John fell into a field of burnt corpses, he could not tell who they were, but somehow, he knew it was those unnamed bodies he had witnessed slaughtered in the rubber field. John walked around the dead, looking at their blackened bodies with no distinguishable features.

One of the burnt hands grabbed John's leg. He stared down in horror as the blackened fingers protruding from the charcoaled flesh squeezed tighter, holding onto his ankle. The skin of the face was burned away revealing eyeless holes lipless teeth in a skeletal grin of death. The jaw fell open and closed, John could feel the corpse trying to say something to him. He bent down to listen closely to what the dead was trying to say.

He was faintly able to make out the sound, "John," the whispered with an eerie intensity, "John."

He opened his mouth to speak but no words would escape his lips.

Again, the body spoke, "John we need to..."

Again, he tried to ask what they needed to do, but his throat refused to produce any words.

"John, we need to go," A booming voice broke him out of his sleep.

It was that of Michael who was standing a couple yards away. John looked and saw that the others were all staring in the same direction, their weapons drawn and aimed behind him.

John arched his head up to find the massive head of the Grootslang lurking directly above him.

Michael moved quickly to grab for John, before he could reach for his friend the thick end of the Grootslang's trunk grabbed Michael by the top of the head. The muscular lip extending from the nostrils protruded over his face getting a firm grasp on Michael. He found himself being lifted off the ground then thrown with a brutal force the likes of which he had never experienced.

Shots were fired, John purposely fell onto his stomach, he attempted to crawl towards the others with bullets flying directly over him towards the monster. A tight force wrapped around his bad leg, when he tried to pull against it the force only tensed harder. His energy drained quickly with the ever-increasing pain rising from his ankle moving throughout his entire body.

John let out a terrible scream, he could feel every inch of the trunk wrapping harder on his leg. Each time it compacted its grip another section of his leg would break sending further coursing pain waiving through him.

John looked towards the others continuing their assault, his vision was fading as his body tried to numb what was occurring to it. He looked for Michael who was lifelessly lying on the ground by a tree, he reached out towards his friend wanting to call for him but found he did not have the ability to produce sound, just like in his dream. The desperation to call for Michael surged, extending his arms out towards the others, John was pulled backwards by his leg. Behind the pain in his lower half he felt an immense weight pressing on top of his lower torso. The increasing pressure began to push his bottom half hard against the ground. Suddenly the force around his leg let go, the sensation of pins and needles covered his injured appendage as blood flowed back into the area. The large muscular trunk wrapped around his chest right under his arms. The impossibly strong tendril tightened like it did with his leg, breaking ribs and squeezing the breath out of him. With each breath he exhaled John found it harder and harder to get air into his lungs, then the beast began to pull. With his lower half pressed to the ground and his upper torso pulled by the trunk, John could feel his insides burning with the most excruciating pain.

He was unable to hear his own scream, the gun shots blasting at the creature atop him were completely muted. The last thing John thought before the life inside him was pulled apart was that there was a fire burning in his abdomen. Then just like that, a euphoric feeling surged through him, and the pleasant thought that maybe Margaret would be making dinner tonight entered his mind as the world around John Alpert faded away.

- - - -

Michael was not fully unconscious after being thrown by the Grootslang but he felt the sensation that he may pass out. His front torso impacted with the ground following the throw, knocking the breath out of him. For what was only a few seconds, but to Michael felt like hours, he gasped for air struggling to fill his lungs. Finally, able to squeeze a quick pant into his chest, Michael rolled to his back watching the others fire round after round in the direction of the beast. As the bullets struck its thick, scaly hide or missed and tore apart the branches around it, Michael watched while the monster pinned his life-long friend to the ground using one of its front legs, then the Grootslang wrapped its trunk around John's chest. What happened next was so haunting, that Michael was positive he hallucinated the incident. Trauma has the ability to make people see things that are not real. Michael prayed that what had happened was just a result of the trauma he had experienced. A world-shattering vision made him wish that the impact had either killed him or knocked him out so that he would have been protected from seeing everything that followed. Every night following would lead him to cry out of a dark slumber, revisiting it for the rest of his life.

The creature pulled John's upper body away from his lower half with the ease of a peeling away a roasted chicken leg from the breast. Michael could do nothing but watch in disbelief as John's body stayed grasped in the hold of the Grootslang. John's dead eyes remained open, a witness of the survivors. Pieces of his spinal column hung down the open gap at his mid-section, with gouts of blood drenching the dirt floor below. The monster's foot held its place on top of the rest of John, the creature's trunk holding his upper half in full display. It was at the moment John's upper intestines, still connected to the rest of his organs, which fell to the jungle floor that broke Michael from his terrorized stupor. The explosive sound of discharged bullets continued to occupy the atmosphere. The click of one of their hammers hitting an empty chamber began to repeat, telling Michael they would soon run out of bullets. Just as dramatically, did the monster make its entrance, it dropped the remains of John. Then turned its immense body around and left the area, leaving them with the aftermath of its presence.

The firing guns were silenced with the exit of the creature. A foggy confusion in the air as not a single person knew how to process what they had just witnessed. No one spoke a word as astonishment connected between the remaining four and all were perplexed at what they should to do next.

Jane was the first to walk off, turning from the others and slowly making her way cutting through the forest. She told herself that Michael and Monroe would need time to allow themselves to collect their thoughts and mourn the terrible loss. She understood, intimately the feeling, especially how hard it was for a loved one to be taken by a divergent entity of the jungle.

Percival was correct in his assessment that the deaths were unnatural, this thing should never have arisen from the depths of the continent. Now, due to its presence, its release was taking a heavy toll on them. Jane was sure that Michael would never recover from witnessing the demise of his friend, she only hoped that he would find solace, in some form, on a supported road to recovery.

Monroe stared blankly at the pieces of what was once John Alpert. The dead face began to grey from the drained blood, lifeless eyes stared up emptily at the ceiling canopy above. Michael was kneeling at the head of his dead friend, tears streaming down his face but he made no sound. Monroe moved over to Michael trying to build the courage to convince the man in continuing their trek. He heard soft whispers emitting from Michael's bent head and quickly understood that he was praying. Even though his parents were missionaries themselves, Monroe never considered himself a deeply religious man. Unable to spiritually connect to the philosophies and beliefs his parents held true. He once joined a missionary prayer group for transport while traveling on assignment, a member of their caravan died from malaria and the priest held a vigil. Monroe, out of respect, attended and listened to the passages read from the texts, the spoken words were meant to ease the transition for the dead in their voyage to the afterlife. Monroe had seen various forms of burial ceremonies and felt that they all aimed for the same goal, the safe passage of the lost from this life to the next.

Now, he looked down at a man he barely knew, but felt oddly closer due to their shared experience, Monroe hoped that Michael was not only praying for John's eternal rest in peace but also for those who remained. He thought he should try and push the thought away, feeling it to be selfish, but in his heart, he felt that John's suffering was over. He was no longer in danger, his fears and pain were over, the four of them were now the ones who had to endure.

After Michael's quiet prayer ended, Monroe put a hand on the Englishman's shoulder signaling it was time for them to go. Michael stood up from his kneeling position, head still bent, wiping the tears away from his face with the palm of his hands. Michael turned to Monroe with red, tearful eyes, he looked as though he wanted to say something. His lips started to tremble with a desperate plea, it pained Michael to leave his friend like this.

What would he say to Margaret when he returned home? How could he justify to her that he had left her brother's body in pieces on the floor of a jungle located in one of the most remote parts of Africa? Michael looked down once more with growing remorse, at this friend's dead face.

"I am sorry John," he whispered.

With that, Michael turned back to Monroe and shook his head in understanding. Presently, the time to mourn needed to be cursory, the danger around them was pressing and the heavy weight of the creature's presence was ever treading on their nerves.

Jane looked back at the others, feeling the fragile optimism breaking if not fully irreparable. Monroe walked shoulder to shoulder with a bleak Michael, Percival looked like a man struggling to hide his own vulnerability.

At the beginning of it all Jane had an instinctual feeling that this group's dynamic would be fatal. It was in her bones that she was to confront the Grootslang but it was assumed this was to be done on her own. Perhaps her hubris was to blame and these men were suffering because she underestimated the monster.

Now that she was able to see the others in their most raw of form, she understood that, possibly, she needed their presence as much as they needed hers. Jane evaluated her own motives as she supposed the others were secretly doing in their minds. She hoped that her quest in stopping the Grootslang would not result in even more death. Jane, over the years, has learned to live with blood on her hands, but all those who died in her company (including her father) understood the risks they were embarking and dove into the fray with glad tidings.

These men though were different, they could never have conceived of the evil they were about to face. She felt responsible for their circumstance and made an oath that no more shall die in her care.

Holding back, Jane waited for Percival to catch up, when the man was within a short distance, she continued walking.

"Being in this low land could be dangerous. Possibly we should head to higher ground," Jane said to him.

The statement was meant to gage the mindset of the hunter, was he back into this fully with her, to help them get out of it or was he too wrapped in his own head to care about the direction they were heading and the steps of survival they should be taking?

Percival's reply sounded indifferent but was exactly what she wanted to hear, "What do you propose?"

"We head over the ridge of that low lying mountain, descending down the other side. It should shorten our path," said Jane pointing towards the area she specified.

"With all due respect Miss Weaver, it makes no difference. Higher ground, lower ground, we are fodder either way," replied Percival.

Jane stopped short and looked the man dead in the eyes, they were cold and empty. She could see he was struggling with something. She needed them all and a man like Percival with honed skills to give her the support she needed, was imperative to pull them all out of this alive.

There are moments in the minds of those with small windows to survival where they must decide to take a chance and press on or lay down and allow the inevitable to occur.

"We are broken, there have been heavy wounds inflicted upon this group. For the sake of survival, we need to stay bounded. If one unravels then we all do, which at that point we may as well stay moored here and allow for that thing to take us," she spoke sternly while maintaining a soft tone.

Percival looked into Jane's deep, penetrating eyes and saw that element of respect that was spoken of each time her name was uttered throughout taverns and drinking holes across the land. It was clear that the resolve that accompanied the name Weaver, coursed through her veins. There are those who spoke of seeing it in her father and here Percival was seeing it burn in the eyes of Jane.

Percival found himself reignited with a surge of hope, "Perhaps we should stay true to course."

Jane curled a corner of her mouth in a half smile, it pleased her to see the man return somewhat, to his former self. Michael would, of course, never be the same and Monroe was too preoccupied with his concern over the well-being of Michael as well as a burning guilt over the death of John.

Jane needed Percival to be level headed. In order for them all to get out of this alive they needed the wits of both hunters to guide them and to pick up the trudge from the other two.

Jane was on full alert. There was a pattern she saw on how the creature would strike. It would result in one of their own being killed then it would instantly draw back, there was no urgency in it to take them all at once. She considered how to predict its actions based upon what she saw, by using her experience and knowledge of predators, she would make an educated assessment of its behavior.

This, of course, was no normal predator which placed it in a category of unpredictability. She had an inclination though that she could call upon its tendencies to push it into a fatal trap. Its rage was one of the Grootslang's most dangerous aspects and Jane thought she knew how to turn that into its major flaw.

XV

They came upon the curve of the mountain where the far end dove into the river valley. A clearing opened before them with its far end dropping down into the lower valley floor where the base of the mountains crashed into each other.

Michael and Monroe stayed near the edge of the jungle as Jane and Percival moved along the opening, looking for any signs of danger. Jane walked over to the point where the trees opened and looked out. The hill before her was very steep, its only plant life, a short grass with dried bushes breaking out in random spots. Four hundred meters down, the jungle teamed hiding the valley floor. Jane looked for signs of the river's edge. The jungle below was dense making it impossible to observe potential paths or clear openings that showed areas for safe travel out.

"Percival," she called to the hunter.

He walked over to her, leaning over to look down the steep decline Percival thought that it was one of the most magnificent sights he had ever seen. After witnessing one of the most horrible monstrosities that Africa held, he forgot that her face was one of the most amazing sights, true gold for the eyes.

Percival pointed down into the thicket of jungle, "Maybe there is a river bend within that valley?"

"Perhaps. I do not care for the dense collection of trees," she stated thinking of the dangers hidden below.

She turned her head to look back towards Michael who was lost in his own thoughts. Monroe, however, appeared to be somewhat back on his normal level of alertness. His attention to their surroundings was constantly distracted by the actions of Michael. She wanted Monroe to stay the course and keep a lookout instead of focusing his attention away from the forest.

"I do not think the risk of descent is merited," Jane said in a quieter tone trying to keep the conversation strictly between herself and Percival.

"One misstep would send a person careening down, colliding those trees," Percival continued in agreement.

Jane began to walk over to Monroe and Michael, the forest by them crashed open and a huge trunk came swinging into view knocking Jane to the ground and shoving Monroe against the closest tree.

The Grootslang stood menacingly over her, they exchanged the same stare as they had before in the darkness of the monster's void. At that moment she was certain it saw her and recognized the danger she posed to its existence. In her peripheral vision, while she locked eyes with the monster, Jane could see Percival running with his rifle in hand. He raised the weapon aiming for a shot but before he could get that shot off the thick trunk reached out striking his rifle which flung back hitting him forcefully in the face. Jane watched as his nose broke open spraying blood down to his mouth and dripping over his chin. The concussion must have knocked him out for Jane saw the hunter fall to the ground with his face implanting in the dirt. She could see that he was alive, and was grateful for that. The only people other than herself capable of coherently firing a weapon were immobile.

Michael was still awake but fell to the ground in a cowering position, the traumatic memory of what had happened to John, combined with the reappearance of the Grootslang, placed him in a catatonic state numbly staring at the monster above. The creature turned its head now looking in the direction of Michael, his feeble condition leaving him open as an easy target. Within seconds Jane watched as it raised one of its front legs threating to stamp with full force on the man. Jane struggled to raise her rifle in firing position discovering her arm was dislocated. Without the ability to use both of her arms to fire at the creature she used her full capable arm to slam the stock of the rifle into the ground embedding it in the dirt. With the weight of the gun held against the ground she used all of her strength to balance the rifle with one hand pointing the muzzle at the Grootslang so it was almost flush against the tusk of the monster.

Seconds before the creature was able to snuff the life out of Michael with one quick stamp, Jane pulled the trigger, firing a shot close range directly at its face. A wave of blood, flesh and ivory exploded, showering Jane with pieces of the sharp white bone, scratching parts of her face. The monster roared in agony, running across the clearing, breaking through the trees opposite her.

Leaving her rifle, Jane pushed herself up off the ground with her one good arm. She walked over to the nearest tree and started to slam her dislocated shoulder against the trunk attempting to knock it back into place. It took three hard tries, each effort accompanied by excruciating pain, but she was able to realign her arm, finally, with one sharp painful pop. Her arm was sore and Jane knew she would not be able to use it to fire her rifle. Options were limited and as Jane looked around at her surroundings, she reminded herself of the creature's rage. It had one predictable response that could be used as a weakness.

Jane ran over to the edge of the clearing at the top of the grassy decent, where she and Percival had stood only seconds before.

Removing her pistol with her good arm Jane patiently waited taking in heavy deep breaths, she flipped open the cylinder checking the rounds then flipped it back in place pulling back the hammer ready to fire.

The beast did not disappoint, emerging once again as expected. Its rage was apparent, the tusk she had hit with her previous shot was almost completely blown off, chunks of flesh and blood dripped from the side of its torn face, the bottom row of flat teeth clearly visible in its lower jaw.

She was not sure if the monster did not see her standing at the far end of the clearing or just ignored her, completely focusing its anger on an easy target, but Jane could see clearly, this time it was looking to charge at the limp body of Percival.

Jane lifted her pistol and began firing shots at the open wound. The beast howled with even more rage locking eyes with Jane once again. With its focus directed on her, Jane widened her stance firing off two more shots striking the monster until it reacted with a loud roar rearing its front legs off the ground extending its body at full length into the air.

The Grootlang then slammed its front legs down onto the ground creating a minor quake and lowering its head, stared directly at Jane. She dropped the pistol and reached for her knife removing it from its sheath holding it reversed grip with the blade facing down. The Grootslang let out one more roar and began its charge, the two never breaking eye contact.

As the beast got closer, Jane stood firming in place eyeing the evil showing no quarter. The monster closed its distance quickly giving Jane no room for error and at the moment before it landed on top of her, Jane took a long step backward permitting herself to fall down the steep hill.

After a few seconds of falling, close to a hundred meters down from where she just stood, Jane took the knife and stabbed the earth, preventing her further decent.

The huge massive body of the Groostlang launched out directly above her with an uncontrolled and wild flailing of limbs and trunk. The monster landed only a couple meters below her boots, its body cascading down the grassy hill until it disappeared into the trees below vanishing from sight. She could hear its cries of rage and pain along with the impactful strikes against the trees as it plummeted deeper into the jungle. Then, as if the earth had opened its mouth and swallowed the Grootslang whole, there was a silence. Jane hung onto the handle of her knife looking down, waiting for any movement or rattle from the trees, to her relief there was none, the forest once again was a still serenity of magnificence.

- - - -

Jane struggled to get back up, her grip on the knife would not be able to hold forever and she was afraid her fate would follow that of the Grootslang, when a thin rope was thrown down to her. She reached out with an intense pain using her bad arm, wrapping the rope around her wrist. When she was secure, she released her knife and grasped the rope with her good hand. The rope began to gradually pull back up lifting her higher until she finally reached the clearing. When she was at the top a set of hands reached out for her pulling her to her feet, she was happy to see that her ascension was made by the combined efforts of Percival and Monroe.

The three of them stood looking down toward the bottom the jungle covering the valley floor. Somewhere down there the body of one of the lands oldest creatures lay dead. The monster was gone, they could finally be at ease.

No one said it, they did not want to inflict an unwanted spell by saying what they already felt.

- - - -

Following two more days of travel, they found an outpost on a British territory near the Belgian border. Percival joined a commercial fishing boat once they reached the settlement. He gave no winded sentimental farewell, just tipped his hat to both Jane and Monroe and was off. Monroe assisted Michael onto their river transport, it would be sometime before Michael could make it home to England. By then Jane secretly hoped he would find a way to come to terms with what had occurred and would be able to live with all that he had lost, but she was doubtful.

On the dock Monroe stepped up to Jane, the hot sun beaming down on her with her hat creating a shadow hiding half of her face.

"You will take care of him, right?" Jane asked.

"I am going to escort him back to England myself. My superiors will be very interested in what I found. What about you, Jane Weaver?" Monroe inquired.

Jane lifted her head making eye contact with Monroe holding a half smile, "I am thinking I will head east, perhaps to Tanga."

Monroe only replied with a big smile, followed by an exchange of handshakes. He turned around to join Michael on their boat as the workers called for the transport to depart.

Jane stood there taking in the sounds and smells, thinking about the people all around. The continent was such a dark mysterious place full of things beyond any outsider's imagination, but what she liked the most were its people. She had seen such evils in her life, those spiritual in nature, and those manmade. But the good in people was what made the land rich and that treasure could not be harvested or stolen.

EPILOGUE

Sonido de la Muerte

The bottom of the valley floor was thick with vegetation, giant trees partially blocking out the sun creating a shadowy atmosphere. Even though the area was dark and full of predators, there were animals calling to each other from all around, each expressing its own pattern of speech and communication.

The broken black body lay unmoving in the darkest part, wedged between two enormous trees. Blood leaked out of the ripped flesh and large gashes, openings bleeding like a dozen slow moving rivers. The body shifted slightly, the forest around hushed in a quick flash of silence. One section bulged out splitting the thick black skin with a black head emerging followed by a long neck. The black eyes with small red dots in the center stared out into the darkness. A forked tongue spit out the mouth tasting the stagnant air sensing all that was around. The serpent slithered out into the jungle to find a place to bide its time.